Somewhere More Than Free

Ed A. Murray

GMB
A Glacier Made Book

A Glacier Made Book.
www.edamurray.com

Originally published in 2015.
Second edition copyright © 2017 by Ed A. Murray

Cover photo by Howard Dansizen. Taken from the public domain.

ISBN: 0-9986889-1-6
ISBN-13: 978-0-9986889-1-6

Printed in the United States of America.

Also by Ed A. Murray

Between Two Slopes

In a Northern Town

"Men are not punished for their sins, but by them."

– Elbert Hubbard

Somewhere

More

Than

Free

For my parents

Book I:

To the Land of Nod

1

Your sins are going to catch up with you. That's what Mason told himself. He was sitting in a hunting blind that he'd built a few years back, not for hunting, but for watching the animals in their natural habitat.

No one else knew about the blind. It was his sanctuary, away from his sanctuary. When he knew he'd have some time to himself, he'd make his way through the forest and climb up into the blind and then just sit there. He'd made a habit of sitting idle. Once you are to a point where the Devil can't possibly do anything more to harm the integrity of your soul, then, Mason figured, it was permissible to sit idly.

For the first few hours he saw nothing but the wind waving

the high branches in the forest, the leaves thick and strong in early August. The woods were green and healthy. In the winter months, Mason could sit in the blind and see for what seemed like miles, his vision piercing through the thin ceiling of the forest until the density of the trees finally won. In the summer, however, it was a completely different ballgame.

It was a cool morning, but Mason knew the day would surely bring with it heat and humidity and so he tried to savor these early hours. Apparently, the predators of the forest thought the same way. The blind was situated high in a tree facing a small clearing, which was oval-shaped and pointed north. Critters of all kinds would make their way through— rabbits, squirrels, porcupines, deer, skunks, birds, foxes— never peeking up to see Mason sitting and observing. He liked the feeling of watching from afar, removing himself from the world. Things tended to go wrong when he got involved.

A lonely white-tailed deer came walking by, cautiously, the way deer tend to walk through the woods, and when it was sure it was safe it bent its head to the forest floor and took a few bites of grass. It wasn't but a moment later that Mason saw the wolf. It was crouched for an attack in the woods, behind the deer. The deer raised its head suddenly and looked around. The wolf remained still. The second the deer lowered its head again the wolf took off. The deer jolted out into the clearing for its escape, but another wolf cut it off and the deer changed direction but then suddenly another wolf appeared and cornered the prey and the deer was suffocated by a hungry pack that seemed to have appeared from the earth itself. The deer never stood a chance.

It wasn't the first wolf sighting that Mason had witnessed, but it was the first time he saw them hunt a deer. It was masterful, such teamwork and precision. The scene caused Mason to think back to two years previous, only a few months after he'd constructed the blind. He was sitting patiently and waiting for wildlife to appear when he saw a deer walk past, just as this one had done. However, as sometimes you can only see from an aerial view, the deer was not alone on that day either. More swiftly than the wolves, a cougar lunged from the underbrush of the forest and took down the deer before it knew it was in danger. The cougar was a marvelous creature, much larger than Mason had ever imagined, with grace and strength all rolled into one powerful attack. Mason thought how lucky he was to have seen the cougar, but then quickly dispelled that notion. He was not a lucky man. He knew that.

He sat in the blind and watched the cougar begin to dig into its well-deserved meal, and that was when he heard the growls. He looked up and saw the wolf pack appearing out of the trees in a united line. There were about seven of them and they showed their teeth and then the cougar showed its teeth as well. When the wolves were close enough the cougar lunged at one of them and swiped its paw and the wolf quickly bounced backward to avoid the blow. The cougar returned to defend its prize and another wolf approached and it lunged again. That's how it went for a few minutes—wolves approaching, daring the cougar, and the cougar then lunging at the wolves to temporarily back them off. If it were one wolf against one cougar, it wouldn't even be fair. But a pack of wolves cornering the giant cat for its prey and the tables turn.

Eventually the stamina of the wolves was too much for the cougar to defend against and the tired cat panted and slumped back into the woods, slowly, defeated.

It was a rare sight, Mason knew, and he was sure to remain quiet throughout the battle, despite his rapid heart rate and his shifting of weight to try to get a better viewing angle. He felt a rush of adrenaline when he watched these scenes play out, and he liked the way it made him feel a little bit scared, like he was in danger himself, but also alive.

When the wolves were done feasting and took the rest of the carcass back to their den to share with the pups, Mason carefully returned to the ground and headed back to his cabin. He knew it was most likely the last time he would see that cougar. When the top brothers of the forest square off, there is a winner and there is a loser. The winner claims stake of the territory, and the loser moves on.

2

The boy was on his own. Fifteen months after his high school graduation and he found himself in a small town on the eastern shores of Lake Michigan. It was a simple and quiet existence, but one that he cherished.

He was originally from the greater Chicago area. The neighborhood where he grew up featured wide streets lined with oversized homes and thick trees with branches that hung overhead to form a natural tunnel. Though not technically identical, all of the homes shared similar qualities. Maybe not twins, but surely close relatives of one another. The boy's house was at the end of a rounded cul-de-sac on a road that sloped downward towards his driveway, which then sloped back upward to the hill upon which the home sat. Someone once told the boy that prior to the house being built, the previous owners had truckloads of dirt delivered so that an artificial hill could be sculpted, on which to build the home so that it sat higher than the neighbors on either side. That was the arrogance that ran rampant in this particular greater Chicago community. That was what the boy grew up witnessing.

Despite having no job, the boy's mother was rarely around. He didn't see her before he left for school, and when he returned to their large home she would still be missing until around dinner time. He never knew where she went, and he certainly never asked. The boy's father was a very powerful man who worked in a large office near the top of a skyscraper downtown. Every morning he wore a fresh suit and carried a briefcase and after he drank one cup of coffee and ate a banana, would climb inside his Lexus and leave. Many nights, the boy would fix his own dinner, as neither of his parents would be home before darkness fell over the neighborhood and he thought it may already be too late to eat a full meal.

That was the life he lived until he graduated from high school. His parents did not attend the commencement ceremony and afterward he went to a friend's house and drank heavily for the first time. They started with spiced rum and Coke, and as the night went on they muscled down a few beers. The boy wasn't wild about the taste but loved the way it made him feel. For the next several months he lay around the house and at night he would drink—sometimes with friends, sometimes alone. Finally over a year out of high school he decided to make a change to his life. He withdrew all of the money from his bank account, which his father had been making contributions to since the boy was a young child, and left town. It would be days until anyone noticed, surely, and the boy rather did not care.

When he drove he started southward and bent around the southern border of Lake Michigan and then headed up the coast for a few hours until he stopped in a little town. He parked his car—a black Chevy Trailblazer from the last year they were in production, a car he bought in spite of his father when the man was too busy to join his son at the dealership—in a lot with a view of the water and turned off the headlights. He began taking short pulls from the bottle of whiskey that he'd brought with him. He did that, looking out at the water and listening to the waves slowly washing onto the sand, until he eventually fell asleep and woke up the next morning to the sun shining against his eyes. The sight of the water in the morning was just as beautiful as it had been the night before, and so the boy decided to stay a second day. That eventually turned into a third, then a fourth, and he should have left the town sooner because the fourth night was when it happened.

—   —   —

He was nineteen and drunk that night.

He'd already spent four days in the town, walking the streets and poking his head into local restaurants for a bite to eat during the day, and then sitting in his car or on a picnic table bench at night while he drank and looked at the lake. The fourth night started no differently.

He was parked in a mostly vacant lot near the beach, facing the water, and he poured a little whiskey into a plastic cup and then walked over to the sand and sat down and watched the sunset. Down the beach to his left there was a family kicking sand, the two little ones were jumping up and down where the water crept to a stop before retreating to the lake. In the other direction a group of teenagers walked together and then setup a small bonfire pit and piled wood to light. The boy could hear the group's laughter all that way down the beach. He sat alone and listened. Happiness resonated from both directions. He remembered his family trips as a young child, back when they still took them, and couldn't muster up one memory that brought a smile to his face. He finished his drink and poured another.

A little while later the sun was completely lost over the horizon and the boy decided he would stay in this town forever. The family to his left was now gone, but the teenagers played music and danced and paired off for walks along the water. Then something startled the boy. A car pulled up quickly in the lot over his shoulder and he looked back at it and realized quickly that it was the police. He tried to bury his cup in the sand, in an effort to conceal his crime, and then stood and headed back to his car. The cops were probably there to keep an eye on the teens, he told himself, but it wasn't worth the risk. He decided to flee.

The road north of town followed the lakeshore for a few miles and then split. To the right was the main road, and to the left was a smaller dirt road that followed the lakefront homes. The boy veered left to stay along the water. The road was too dark to see very well, cutting through thick woods. His headlights allowed him to see the occasional driveway on the left, but trees as deep as he could see were on the right. His anxiety kept him glancing in the rearview mirror to watch for cops, but he was in the clear. That's what he continued to tell himself. The radio was playing quietly, but he just listened to his own thoughts. Keep a clear mind, you're not that drunk, he told himself. Just find a place to tuck away and park for the night. He glanced in the mirror behind him again but it was all black. When he returned his eyes to the road he caught himself drifting to the right and driving too fast. He tried to correct the wheel but it was too late. It all happened so quickly, he couldn't react. The wheels slid on the dusty road surface and then he thought he heard someone scream. A loud thump and he was pressing the break with all his strength and the car was fish-tailing and the airbag had deployed into his chest and he couldn't see anything. And then when the car came to a stop it was silent.

3

When Mason first came to Marquette, the old man, who he now called Jones, asked, "You lookin fer Nod?"

Mason was confused and decided not to answer. They were standing outside a gas station convenience shop. Mason sat down on top of a picnic table nearby and the old man remained standing. They were looking out at the road as cars sparsely passed. Mason was in bad shape, and the old man must have seen it.

"Yer just wanderin, right?" Jones asked.

Mason nodded.

"You'd be surprised how many of you we have. Not many folks choose this town. They just stumble upon it and then they stay. First it's just fer a couple days and then they blink and it's thirty years."

"Well you can bet it's just a couple days for me," Mason told the old man.

That was six years ago.

— — —

Thick woods surrounded a small field where Jones owned two homes.

The first was a two-bedroom log home with wood so dark it looked moist and a stove pipe poking from the corner of the roof where a thin trail of smoke often appeared. There was a simple porch built off the front of the home that faced the field and Jones sat in his rocking chair on each pleasant day and looked out at the land. A single dirt road cut through the pasture. The field had obviously come first, and then when the human invasion came, as it always did to beautiful places, the road was laid right on top of the grass. The road started across the way in the woods and ended beside Jones's place. It also served as his driveway.

A little way down the tree line was a second cabin where Mason resided. It was a tiny structure that sat at the base of a sloping hill, with dry wood on its outside and was just as poor inside. The front of the cabin looked out, not at the field, but sideways to Jones's place, so the old man could always keep an eye on it. The rear of the cabin nestled into a curve in the hill so that two of its sides were barricaded from the sun. The overhanging trees, which grew diagonally from the soil of the sloping hill, would litter its seeds and leaves and twigs onto the roof so that once a month in the summer and fall Mason would have to climb up on top and sweep the shingles clean.

It was a simple and humble living but that's how Mason wanted to live. He used the lifestyle as a warranty for clearing his mind. If you physically remove yourself from devastation, you can become a new man. That was all Mason wanted to accomplish. When he first arrived in Marquette six years ago, he sold his junky Trailblazer and got a job working landscaping for a few local fellas. Over the course of a few months he let his brown hair grow out and now he pulled it back on his head and hid it under a baseball cap. For the first time in his life he built calluses on his hands and he added strength to his formerly wiry frame. He no longer felt like a boy. It was a self he never could have imagined as a child.

One morning Mason emerged from the woods in the early evening and walked back to his cabin. He could feel the perspiration congregating in the center of his back and sliding down to the top of his jeans. He removed his cap and wiped his forehead with the back of his forearm and when he looked at his arm he saw he'd smeared three mosquitoes on the sweaty, hairy surface. As he neared his place, he glanced over to Jones's cabin. The old man stepped out onto the porch when he saw the young man approaching and he waved his arm and then leaned his weight onto the wooden railing.

"Boy," Jones called. "You stoppin fer dinner?"

"What are you making?"

Jones gave him a look.

"I can eat."

"Run out fer some brew, will ya?" the old man said.

Mason nodded. "Before dinner?"

"Y'think I wanna eat without brew?"

It was a dumb question on Mason's part, he knew that. So he said, "I'll get it," and then kept walking.

Before heading to the store, Mason went inside his cabin to change into a dry shirt. He loved stepping inside that place. There was a natural piney smell that never seemed to fade, and it was always dark inside unless he decided to click on a few lights. In his bedroom, he grabbed a shirt from the closet and threw it over his head. He tossed the sweaty shirt into a small hamper beside the door and it sat right on top, reminding him how behind he was on his laundry. There was just never any urgency to get it done.

He was about ready to run to the local market so he could make it back in time for dinner with Jones, but before doing so he felt compelled to slide open the small drawer built into his nightstand. Inside there was a rosary and a Bible. Poking from inside the Bible was a faded, nearly brown piece of paper. He removed it and stared at it closely. It was a newspaper clipping, dated six years in the past. Mason had a difficult time looking at the images on the paper, but he had just as difficult of a time avoiding them. A guilt flooded his body, as it always did, and his heart beat faster and he tried to blink away a stinging behind his eyes. The face of a teenage girl stared back at him. He'd never seen her in color, but he could tell she had deep blue eyes and wavy blond hair and a beautiful smile. He tried to force himself to remember the last moment, but it was forever blurry in his memory. How he wished to see it clearly. The guilt. The regret. The pain. He wanted to die. He hadn't lived since that night. Maybe he was dead already.

Tucking the clipping back inside the Bible, he said a quick prayer and looked up to the ceiling to push it to God, the forgiving Lord.

—   —   —

The drive to the market was about fifteen minutes. Mason kept the windows rolled down and he could feel the humidity hanging in the air as the temperature dropped. Clouds had rolled in on the day as it turned to evening and a storm was coming.

He pulled his cap down lower on his head and tried to clear his mind. But all he could think about—all he ever thought about—was that face.

A little while down the road he finally came to the market. He parked his car and went inside, grabbed a case of Bud Light from the fridge and paid at the counter.

The market is at the intersection of two roads with a four-way stop. Cars don't generally come to a complete stop, as there aren't many other drivers on the road, so they just roll through and keep going. When Mason walked back out to his car, this same act occurred. He tossed the case of beer on the passenger's seat and then glanced up at a black Ford Escape slowing down as it approached the stop sign. It was a very ordinary moment—the kind of moment that happens thousands of times every day, the kind of moment he never stops to think twice about. It was the kind of moment that would have passed, and then rather than fading somewhere into Mason's distant memory, it would have simply vanished altogether as if it never even existed. That is, until the blond-haired girl in the passenger's seat turned her head for a brief moment and locked eyes with Mason. He froze. The Ford sped off through the intersection and disappeared around a corner down the road.

It was her. The girl he killed six years ago.

4

He didn't know where the bulk of his guilt originated: committing the crime in the first place, or the fact that he'd seemingly gotten away with it.

He drove slowly back toward his cabin to deliver the beer, but he couldn't stop thinking about that face. It was her. He'd looked at that photo a million times. He saw her in his sleep—in his nightmares. For a moment he thought about quickly hopping in his car and chasing her down. But he was still frozen. It couldn't have been her, he told himself, but then he thought again that he was positive. But it was impossible. A figment of his guilt.

As he drove he couldn't feel his body. He couldn't feel his

hands gripping the wheel nor his foot pressing the pedal. Adrenaline pumped down his arms and legs, but he couldn't feel his heartbeat. That girl wasn't imagined. She was real, but she was in heaven. Then he thought, you're not going to heaven so you'll never see her again. So that couldn't have been her. But it was. But it couldn't have been.

Eventually he pulled out of the woods and into the open field and let gravity slow the car down the road that ended between Jones's cabin and his. He parked and just stared out the windshield at the massive hill beyond the homes with all the trees growing out of its side. His mind was in a bad place.

Doing his best to regain his composure, he grabbed the case of beer and headed inside. The comforting scent of a fresh meal filled the air. The old man was just getting ready to sit down at the table. There were bowls set in the middle and two plates with a knife and fork set before two chairs. Mason glanced in the bowls and saw cornbread in one and asparagus in the other. Jones walked up and placed a tray of chicken breast down on the table and looked up at Mason.

"Got the brew?" It was a rhetorical question, as Mason held the case with both arms right in front of him.

"Right here." Mason opened the box and placed two beers down on the table, and then stuck the box in the fridge.

Mason must not have been as composed as he'd hoped, because the old man said, "You look like you seen a ghost, boy."

He ignored the comment and headed back over to the table where Jones was already sitting down and beginning to pile food onto his plate. Mason watched the old man, who was now pushing eighty, who still had a full head of hair albeit as white as a clean blanket of winter snow. Jones was a large man in his day, but strength fades with age and now as he sat, the skin on his cheeks and arms sagged and jiggled with each movement. He could still get around pretty well, that wasn't a problem, but the man was long since retired and was only as active as he needed to be.

"What's new with you?" Jones asked.

Mason shook his head, as if to say "nothing" but was still thinking about the girl. She was all he could think about.

"Tell me, it's been about six years now, huh?"

This time Mason nodded. "I think that's about right." He thought for a quick moment. "Six years this month, actually." He heard the words come from his mouth and then he thought about the evil that surrounded this month, the anniversary of the worst night of his life. He hated August.

"Well I'll be." The man's plate was now full and he picked up his fork and knife and began cutting pieces of chicken. "What's next for you in this life?"

"I'm just taking it one day at a time." Mason reached across the table and started serving himself.

"You can only do that so long. Time comes you gotta start lookin ahead. Yer still young. What, twenty-four?"

Mason nodded. "Well, twenty-five."

"Twenty-five, shit, and still slummin around in a cabin in the middle of nowhere."

"I like it here."

"Well you sure's shit don't act like it." Jones took a short break. He sipped his beer and then shoved two pieces of chicken into his mouth. He was chewing with his mouth open and didn't even wait to swallow before continuing to talk. "What are you, runnin from somethin? Yer young and got yer life ahead still."

Mason didn't respond. He was looking down at his plate and moving food around with his fork. The old man must have seen the concern and thoughts running through his mind.

"I ever tell you how I came to this town?"

"A few times, yeah."

"Well I'm tellin ya again. I was probably about yer age— yer age now, not when you showed up here. I was lookin fer any work I could find. Back when I came here, this place was even more in the middle of nowhere than it is today. Hard to believe, I know. But it was exactly what I was lookin fer. Probably the same fer you, right?" He gestured at Mason, who just stared back at the man.

Jones must have seen the uneasiness in the boy's face and ended his story there. Mason looked back down at his food and finally took a bite. Then he cracked open his beer and took a long drink from the can. He could feel it bubbling all the way down. It wasn't very often that he drank. Not anymore. Not since that night.

The two continued eating in near silence and Jones finished first and stood up and walked his plate over to the sink.

A minute later Mason finished his as well and did the same, and then he helped Jones pack up the leftovers and put them into the fridge. Mason pocketed a couple more beers and then thanked Jones for the meal. Just as Mason pushed on the door to head back to his cabin, he heard the old man say something that caught him by surprise. He stopped dead.

"You can't outrun yer past."

Mason looked back at the old man, who was now walking over to the couch in an adjacent room. "What?"

"Live yer life as best you can, is all."

With that, Mason turned and headed home. When he got there he found a chair at the kitchen table and set the beers down in front of him. One by one, he opened them and drank. They tasted immaculate. When they were gone, he went over to a cabinet and grabbed a bottle of whiskey that still had its seal intact—he'd nearly given up drinking altogether. Now his willpower was diminishing. He poured half a glass and drank the poison like water, taking full gulps instead of casual sips. The burn lasted all the way down his throat and settled in his stomach. When it wore off, he took another. He sat in his chair and the world sat silently with him. Until his mind began spinning. He thought about the girl, the one he killed, the one he saw in town. She had the wavy hair he'd imagined. She was beautiful, as he knew she'd be. But she wasn't really there. Not possible. She was a vision of his guilt, his conscience playing jokes on him. Evil jokes. Evil jokes for an evil human being.

When the glass was empty Mason poured another, and then another and emptied the bottle. He drank those two quicker than the first and then he stood up and clutched the armrest on the chair with both hands to keep himself standing. Blinking rapidly, he tried to find some balance. He took a step forward and his weight tipped the chair and it fell over onto the floor and Mason toppled on top of it. He rolled off and smacked himself in the face and tried to shake the drunk from his eyes. He was in bad shape. Lying on his back in the middle of the floor, he could see the girl floating above him, staring down and smiling so gently. He flailed his arms pathetically to shed the image from his mind.

A moment later he was driving down the road. He glanced in his rearview mirror for cops and he blinked some more and he shook his head and this time he saw the girl walking on the side of the road, and she turned and smiled at him again and he suddenly had complete control of the car and continued steering towards her, accelerating, and her smile never faded as the front end of the vehicle plowed into her.

And a little while later Mason opened his eyes, which were now working again, and he lifted himself off the floor and set the chair back up. There was vomit down the front of his shirt. He sat back down and saw that the bottle was empty and he clutched his head, for a slight throb had begun that he knew would only worsen. And then he thought about her again.

5

It was a long night for Mason, and when he awoke he was lying on the couch in his underwear. He sat up and looked for his shirt but then left it wherever it was on the floor and went to the bathroom.

When he returned to the living room, he pulled back the shades and saw the sun was landing over the trees and into the pasture, which meant it was later in the day than he'd planned on sleeping. Thus, he began hurrying through his morning routine, and when he was dressed and out the door with his coffee in hand he saw that he had a voicemail. He listened to it as he climbed into his car and added the old sunfaded cap to his outfit. It was from his boss, a stern man named Terry who suffered from a Napoleon complex. In a frustrated tone, Terry left Mason the directions to a new job. Mason noted the address on a loose receipt he had in his center console and followed the roads for miles until they took him out onto a narrow pass that trailed along the shores of Lake Superior. Houses lined the road to his right and as he passed them he could glimpse views of the vast lake between the homes.

At the noted address there was a tall mailbox at the road. Mason pulled up beyond it and parked his car and proceeded up the driveway toward the house. He had seen Terry's old truck parked as well, with the trailer full of tools and supplies, so he knew he'd found the right house. As Mason walked up the driveway, the shrubs lining the front yard opened up on the left and the magnificent home sat proudly, its white painted wood siding and light blue shutters looked brand new. The driveway bent at the end into a circle drive by the front porch, but if one were to continue straight off the concrete he would find himself on a sloping hill with thick grass that gradually descended to the rocky shores of the lake. That's where Mason saw Terry and two other contractors already hard at work.

When Terry saw Mason approaching he waved him down and then wiped the sweat from his forehead while he waited. He was leaning on a shovel catching his breath, his barrel chest heaving, as Mason stepped up in front of him.

"Jesus, an hour late," Terry said.

Mason didn't say anything, he was busy looking at the land, and then the water over Terry's shoulder, and then at his boss's short hair that he was somehow able to keep slicked back with enough hair gel to last a month.

"Listen, boy," Terry said, taking his weight off the shovel and stepping toward his tardy employee. "This here is a new client we got here. Don't go messin this up fer the rest of us, ya hear?"

"What's the job?"

"Fixin this whole place up." Terry extended his arm as if casting an imaginary blessing over the lawn. "The man wants that there flattened, and we'll line that with stones. Then that there will need to be mulched and we're puttin in steps down there off the patio." Terry pivoted to face the lake and then motioned with his arms, as if directing an airliner. "We'll put a path right here down this hill all the way to the water."

"Shit, that's a lot."

"Shit is right, but we're gonna get it done, ya hear?"

"Yes, sir."

"Gigs like this need constant maintenance, if you know where my head's at, kid. This one could pay out several times."

"I'll go grab a shovel."

"And then join those two clowns over there."

Mason began to head back to the trailer by the road, and as he did he glanced up into an upstairs window and saw a face looking down at him. It was her again. And she smiled and then disappeared.

6

For the rest of the afternoon, Mason didn't go five minutes without stealing a peek back up into that window. Each time it was empty. His mind was spinning and at first he thought it was the heat, and then he thought it was the hangover, and then maybe that he didn't drink enough coffee.

Out over the lake they could see the sun was already past its afternoon peak.

"Alright, boys, good work today," Terry hollered, and the two men Mason was working beside set their shovels against a nearby tree and headed back up the drive. Terry was on the driveway as well and called to Mason, "Don't be late tomorrow," and then turned back toward his truck as well.

Mason took a deep breath and before retreating for the day he walked down the slope to the water. He crouched low and submerged his hands. The cold rush of Superior entered in his fingertips and tingled its way up his arms. Then he cupped some water and splashed it onto his face. He felt his lungs hesitate for a brief moment and then he caught his breath. He removed his hat and dumped another splash of water over his head and ran his fingers through his hair before returning his cap. He did this a few more times and he could feel the heat leaving his body altogether.

Content with drips of cold water still running down his body, beneath his shirt and into his jeans, he stood and turned back toward the house. The patio off the back of the house sat several yards above the lawn and looked out over its domain. From down by the water, the patio looked even more majestic. Just then, a young woman stepped out of the sliding glass door and onto that patio and sat down on a lawn chair. She had a white towel draped over her shoulders and her sunglasses covered nearly half her face. She set down a book on the table beside her and then removed the towel. Underneath she wore a yellow and white bikini with thin strings that tied around her neck and on either hip. She was rubbing sunscreen on her arms and legs when she must have noticed Mason. She paused and her glare shook him from his stare and he began walking back up the lawn. The entire walk he stole glances and as he came up beside the patio, so that his shoulders were level with

the surface, he found himself saying out loud, "Sorry if I startled you." Immediately he was embarrassed for speaking and
continued walking.

"It's okay," he imagined her saying in reply.

When he looked back at her, he thought he saw her looking
at him and then sliding her sunglasses on top of her head, re-
vealing beautiful blue eyes—just as Mason had always imagined. The girl. He froze and he wanted to look away and then
run but his legs wouldn't work and then he thought he might
vomit. He must have winced, as if in pain, though he couldn't
feel anything. She was real. No she wasn't.

"Are you okay?"

He breathed heavily. "Yep." She's real. No she's not.

"You're with the landscapers," she said, as if fact, as if she
knew everything about him already. Of course she did. He'd
killed her. She'd probably been haunting him for six years and
knew everything about him.

"Yep," he said again. "You're—" he started, but then
stopped. "New to town?" he finished as a question.

"You could say that." She stood and took a step toward Mason, but he flinched and she stopped.

"I'm sorry, I have to go." And he left.

7

He didn't remember driving home that night. Suddenly he was just parked beside the cabin and Jones was sitting on the porch staring at him, like old men do. Jones had a reserved nature about him and he seemed to be a statue.

Mason parked his car and got out and as he turned toward his cabin he watched Jones for a moment. He was sipping coffee and his lower lip protruded in a very specific spot, and then he brought his lips to the mug and spit into it and Mason realized the old man was dipping, not drinking evening coffee. Then he heard Jones call to him.

"Dinner, boy?"

"Nah."

Mason went inside and shut the door behind him and allowed himself to collapse against the closed door and slide down to the floor. He sat there for several minutes without making a sound. He could hear the old refrigerator unit in the kitchen click on and rumble for a few minutes and then shut itself back off. There were a couple eerie creaks that seemed to come from the drying floorboards beneath him, but he ignored them and reasoned them to the unknown.

For the next half hour he remained on the floor. He couldn't shake the image of the girl from his mind. He thought about how she stepped toward him. There was a soft, flowery scent that had wafted his way. It was all in his mind. Her hair flowed and the light breeze had tickled it into stray waves. It was all in his mind. Her voice though—he had heard that clearly, he had responded. He spoke to her. But it was all in his mind.

Eventually the sun disappeared on the day and Mason finally stood from the floorboards and reached for a lamp to bring light into the cabin. Then he walked over to the cabinet and retrieved a bottle of whiskey. He poured a few fingers into an empty cup that was sitting on the counter, but he left it sitting there. Be strong, he continued telling himself. He didn't know what to do. For the last six years he had been living in a cloudy nightmare, but he had learned to live there and had become content in that nightmare. Acknowledging his guilt, remaining as solitude as possible and continuing to wake each morning was his only routine. That was his normal. In the beginning, this new lifestyle was a necessity. Then it became contentment. Then it became complacency. And then the Devil recognized his complacence and took advantage of it by taunting his sins before him.

Not once in the last six years had Mason thought about returning home. Telling his parents he was sorry. Hoping they would allow him to move back in, start over. He was no longer a boy now. He was a man, and men aren't forgiven so easily. Mason twisted on the kitchen faucet and splashed a cupped handful of cool water on his face. He held his head over the sink for a moment and breathed heavily as his lungs adjusted to the sudden rush of cold. He opened his eyes and watched the remaining water drip from his face and make small splashes on the porcelain surface.

That's when her face reappeared in his mind. Go away, he thought. Go away. I've paid enough for this sin. I will continue paying for it until the Lord claims my soul—until my soul is claimed, he corrected himself. He was far from convinced the Lord would be the one to claim it. Then he thought, just confess. Go to the authorities and tell them the truth, what you've done. Then he thought no, that won't do any good. No man can judge you now. You answer to Him only.

Why did she have to be beautiful. Damn it, he was picturing her face again. Mason pushed himself back from the sink and walked into the bedroom and grabbed his Bible. He flipped it open and looked at the girl's face again. That was her. He was sure of it. She appeared to him twice now. That was her. That was her. Damn it, that was her. He cringed and closed the Bible for a moment and looked to the sky to try to keep any tears from spilling. Then he looked at the article again. He saw her name—Chloe. She was an innocent girl and he killed the innocence and everything that was good in the world. What was left to do? He could escape again, go live in the woods in his tree blind and watch the wolves and cougars fight it out over their prey. He could move out West, find a small place to live somewhere between desert and mountain and drink water from a nearby stream and kill his own food.

The only thing he knew for sure was that this life had gone terribly wrong. He was destined for much more, and then one day his life ended and he began trudging through these endless days and nights of breathing and thinking and slowly dying.

That was her. No it wasn't.

Mason walked back into the kitchen and picked up the glass of whiskey that he'd poured a few minutes earlier and took a long, painful drink.

— — —

The next day nothing had changed. She was on his mind when he first awoke, and during the drive back to the house and even once the work began he continued thinking about her and looking up at the empty window. The events of that night replayed in his mind and every time his shovel crunched into the dry soil he flinched and squeezed his eyes shut.

One of the other workers took notice of his apparent pain and confusion and asked if he was okay.

"I'm fine," was all Mason offered. The other two men went back to work and Mason looked out at the calm lake rolling in to shore, and then back at the house. He leaned his forearm on the end of his shovel. "You guys ever see a girl at this place?"

"This house?" one said, nodding toward the large mansion while continuing to displace the dirt.

Mason nodded. "I thought I saw a girl here."

"I ain't seen her," one of the men said. He didn't even look up from his work.

"Me either," said the other. "Met the man though. Nice guy. Says his wife made him buy this place."

"Oh poor man, has to live in a place with this view."

"That's what I'm saying."

Mason ignored the two men and went back to digging, continuing to glance back at the house. A little while later one of the men turned back to him, just as he'd begun to distract himself from his own thoughts, and said, "But no, I ain't seen a girl here."

—   —   —

They were sitting in the shade of a tree at the top of the sloping yard drinking lemonade and eating turkey sandwiches. Mason wiped the sweat from his forehead and down his temples with the neck of his shirt. The lemonade was too sweet for him and he poured some out into the grass and added some water to it.

"So what did this girl look like?"

"Huh?" Mason said.

"The girl you asked about earlier. Is she cute?"

"I didn't see a girl," he lied, though he wasn't actually sure if he was lying. "Just wondering if there was one around."

"You just randomly asked if we saw a girl here, no reason for it?"

"Yep."

"Yer a strange dude."

They ate a little more and when Mason finished his sandwich he laid back onto the lawn and felt the sun warm his skin. It felt nice when he wasn't moving. A swirling breeze skimmed off the water and trickled up his arms and nullified the sun's kiss.

"So what's yer deal?" one of the men asked.

"What do you mean?"

"Yer just a quiet dude. I just don't know why yer livin in the UP, I guess. If I were you, I'd take my ass to California er something."

"I just like it up here. God's country, you know? Kind of refreshing when you come from miles and miles of concrete."

"Sure," the man said. "Listen, I been here twenty-nine

years, which means I ain't bullshittin you when I say no one likes it here."

Mason sat up and looked at him. "It works for me."

"Shit, the only thing this place works for is cuttin yerself off from the rest of civilization."

8

The remainder of the day followed the same trend. Mason and the other two men continued working, staying on pace, and every few minutes Mason would look up into the window and see the sun's glare with nothing behind it.

Around six o'clock the men were packing up and Terry parked his truck and greeted them. He looked around the yard with his hands on his hips, evaluating.

The lawn running up to the back patio and along a line of trees had been churned. Against the patio the three men had built up a floral bed with heavy square stones and planted greenery and flowers all throughout. To the right the bed sloped down to the lawn's level and the men littered the bases of the trees with mulch and added a small stone border with large stone steps that weaved in and out of the trees all the way down to the water.

"Lookin good, boys," Terry said. "Think you can finish this up tomorrow?"

"Don't see why not," one of the men said.

"Good. I told the owner three days so get it done."

Terry went back to his truck and pulled away and Mason lingered, hoping to find some evidence that he wasn't hallucinating, but none surfaced. Then again, none could surface, because he knew he was hallucinating, and the circle of inner turmoil continued like that as he slowly drove himself mad.

Finally he left and drove home slowly and calmly and began to fade into a comatose state. As he passed the final corner store before veering off the main road and back into the woods, he stopped and picked up some beer to take over to Jones. The shop was out of Bud Light so Mason decided it wouldn't hurt to change things up, get Miller Lite this time. He bought the beer and returned to the cabin.

As was the case on most days, Jones was sitting on the front porch watching Mason as he pulled up. Mason looked at the old man, who nodded to him and said, "Ten minutes work fer you?"

"Works great."

It was enough time for Mason to go inside and change clothes, splash some water on his face and take a shot of whiskey. It went down smoothly and he contemplated taking another, but the better part of him advised against it and he instead grabbed the case of beer and walked next door.

Jones was watching TV, the volume turned nearly to mute. Two cowboys raced aggressively through a dusty plain, clouds stirring behind their broncos as they sprinted. The men bounced and grimaced at one another but nonetheless rode silently. Mason couldn't tell if they were supposed to be friends or enemies.

"What have you there?" Jones asked over his shoulder.

"Beer."

"What is it?"

"Miller Lite."

"No Bud?"

"They were out."

The old man breathed deeply and then clicked off the TV. "Bud sold out," he seemed to say to himself. "I s'pose beer is beer." He stood and walked over to the kitchen and then carried two dishes to the old wooden table. Mason followed behind, unloaded the beer into the refrigerator and then brought two back with him to the table. Jones had already taken a seat and Mason slid him a beer and then sat down across from him.

The two began eating—grilled chicken, carrots and homemade bread. The only sound was chewing and breathing and the occasional knife slicing across a plate. Mason looked up at the old man, who cracked open his beer and took a foamy first slurp out of the can, and then he waited for a response. Jones had a stoic look on his face and he placed his hands on the table and sat up straight.

Mason raised his eyebrows. "So?"

"Like I said, beer is beer." Jones took another sip. Mason was relieved—he had yet to bring home beer for Jones that wasn't one of his go-to brands. He took a breath and looked away, but when his eyes lingered back to Jones the old man still didn't look particularly pleased. "When you try somethin new, two things can happen," he continued. "It goes good, er it doesn't."

Mason waited. "And which case is this?"

"This is beer, so that don't apply. That always ends good." And then Jones smirked and took another long gulp and continued eating his chicken. Mason did the same and another word wasn't spoken at the table until their plates were empty.

When they were finished eating, they both just sat and looked around the room. Then Jones said, "You remember what you told me when you came to this town?"

He shook his head.

"You told me you'd be here just a couple days."

"Yep."

"You know how long ago that was?"

"Six years."

"Six years," Jones said. "Six damn years."

Jones was staring at Mason, waiting for a response, but when Mason looked into the old man's eyes he couldn't find the strength to stare back and instead he let his eyes wander the room. A couple years ago—hell, a few days ago—Mason would have stared the old man down and told him in a stern voice that he knew exactly what he was doing with his life. But times had changed and so had Mason, and now he wasn't exactly sure where his life was heading.

When Jones saw the boy wasn't going to say anything, he continued speaking. "Yer smart, I know yer smart. What are you doin here?"

"Livin my life. I don't see anything wrong with what I'm doin."

"Ain't nothin wrong? Shit, boy." Jones pushed back from the table and stood and walked back into the kitchen to rinse his plate in the sink.

Mason slouched and hung his shoulders. His mind was all over the place. He wanted to think about the girl—Chloe, she had a name, he told himself. But then there was the old man, who had taken him in and treated him like a grandson, and he wanted to listen to the man's words and abide by his wisdom. Old men have a funny way of captivating a conversation. Jones was no exception. Maybe it was his burly size. Or maybe his gravelly voice or just his authoritative tone. Whatever it was, Mason wanted to listen, but his mind was elsewhere, trying to decide if he was still sane, if he was being haunted by his sins, and if he deserved to live with them or die for them. Then the old man spoke.

"You know, in six years you never asked me how I wound

up in this town."

"I thought you always lived here," Mason confessed. "Or at least someplace near here."

Jones shook his head and then turned away from the sink to face the boy. "It's been six years and you don't know my story," he said plainly. "Well, it's about time I tell it."

Mason waited patiently at the table. Jones grabbed two more beers from the fridge and waved the boy over to the living room. Jones sat in his old faded beige swivel rocker and Mason took a seat on the couch. They each opened a beer and took a sip and then Jones began his confession.

"I fucked up."

Mason waited. He saw Jones gauging his reaction to the statement.

"You ever hear of a town called French Lick, down in Indiana?"

Mason shook his head and took another sip.

"Of course you haven't. That's where I'm from." The old man kept pausing, as if he didn't know where to begin. As if he were figuring out how to best word what he'd say next. His eyes were glossy but no tears fell. That's just how old men were. "You ever been in love, boy?"

"Not me," Mason said, and it was the truth. He had obsessions, but he didn't have love. There were moments when he tried to convince himself that he could live again, really live, go out and meet a girl and get on with life. But in the end, her face showed up in the front of his mind and he always stayed put.

"I was in love. Her name was Charlotte. Me and Charlotte went way back to when we were just youngins. That girl had the prettiest eyes you ever seen, and legs like you wouldn't believe. Somehow I got that girl to marry me. This was back, way back when I was just a kid, little younger than you."

"Life was good," Mason said, and he wasn't sure if it was a statement, a question or just a wish.

"Damn right life was good. Until one day it wasn't." Jones took a break, and then said, "You gotta understand this is a story I ain't told in a long time."

The boy nodded.

Then Jones looked him right in the eye with the most serious look Mason had seen in six years, and said, "You get yerself one of them in this life, you don't give her up."

"Yes, sir."

"I got to drinkin, you see. Thought it was fun and good, til it started to get the better of me. One night I come home, I sees her sittin there and I just go off—just go off. No real good reason. Start hollerin about the dishes er somethin. She starts cryin and what not, and I smack her. So she started cryin and holdin her face, and I smack her again. I kept doin it. I couldn't help it. I was mad and I couldn't tell you why." Jones took a long drink from the can and looked out the window. He looked like this time the tears may actually fall. "That was it. She wanted me gone and I think so did I. I took off, wound up here somehow and never left. Worst part—I gave up drinkin, tried to straighten myself out and go back and get her. But it didn't happen. I just kept seein myself as evil. The fact I laid hands on the woman I loved. There ain't no undoin that."

Mason didn't know what to say. He wanted to give the old man the chance to say everything he had to say. But when it looked like the story may have been over, Mason simply said, "I'm sorry."

"Don't be. I did it myself. Ain't no one else I can blame." Jones finished the first beer and opened the second. "I went back to drinkin, obviously. Figured if there ain't no goin back, may as well try to numb myself a little."

The story saddened Mason. This was a man he had gotten to know. When you see the whole picture, things change. People aren't always who you think they are. But Mason's mind once again quickly distracted from Jones and wandered back to his own situation, and he realized that just like the old man he may be stuck like this forever—wandering, never finding a home, just looking for the next place that's not real life.

Then Jones spoke again, regaining Mason's attention. "You know why I tell you this story?"

"Not really."

"I can't help but figure you got yerself in a similar situation. I don't want to see a boy yer age throwin his life away so young."

"You did it."

"You and me ain't the same, boy. I was evil, you ain't."

"You don't know that."

"Well I certainly pray you ain't. See, there's good men in this world and there are men that ain't no good. That's just the way it is. So if there's any chance yer a good one, you gotta get out while you still can."

Mason pretended to ponder what kind of man he was, though he already knew. What he really needed to ponder was whether or not he should disclose his secret to his friend. It seemed that after Jones's story, the old man would understand—or at least sympathize with his sin. But not a soul on earth knew the truth. It was between Mason and God—and Satan.

Then Jones finished by saying, "Evil has a way of followin a man," and Mason agreed, thanked the old man and left.

9

Six years was a long time to get to know someone. In all those days, Mason had come to know Jones not as a landlord, but as a good friend and as a mentor. It was interesting to Mason, sometimes, how you end up befriending someone who is so similar to you that you may share the same soul—and the same sins. It gets to the point where you have to decide if that likeness is a good thing or a bad thing.

He thought about that as he clutched the bottle of whiskey. But his mind couldn't stay on track long, because in a moment it was back on the girl, on his own sins, and Jones was just the fading past in the cabin next door. He poured a shot into a whiskey glass and took it, and then he poured another. As he drank, his vision faded but the memory of the girl strengthened. She was right there before him. Her hair was wavy and she teasingly played with a stray strand. She was wearing a tight top and jeans and she was walking toward him, smirking, staring, and her hips switched from side to side.

Mason lay on his couch, staring at the ceiling and imagining the scene. He wanted to snap out of it, but he couldn't. He needed a distraction. The only outlet at his disposal would be to leave. The initial thought was to bring the bottle into the woods, trek his way to the blind and climb the tree and sit at the top of the forest. But he had a tightness in his breathing and he became anxious, and as he drank another shot he thought he needed to know the truth. So instead of the woods, he grabbed the bottle and his keys and decided to drive.

The winding roads seemed strange and unfamiliar and he felt like he was driving way too fast and after a while he thought he was suddenly back in that night. He felt himself glancing in his rearview mirror and he thought he might whip his eyes back to the road and see her walking, and maybe this time he could swerve in time. He continued driving like this, probably uneasily with his car swaying from shoulder to the middle median, and a few paranoid minutes later he finally eased to the side of the road and put the vehicle in park. The night felt uncommonly still and he rolled down his window and the cool night air rushed inside and he took a deep breath to fill his lungs and he could breathe again.

When he looked up, he was parked outside of the house

where he had worked the previous two days. Shutting off the engine, he slouched down in the driver's seat and took a deep breath. You're losing it, just keep it cool, he told himself. What the hell are you doing? Showing up at this house? You knew where you were going the whole time.

A nightly fog was beginning to fall over the community and it hovered a few feet off the ground. His window was now down and he stuck his arm out and felt the cool moisture that swept in off the lake. The air was mostly still and offered no friction for the noises of the night. Crickets chirped in a patch of tall grass. He thought there might be a few frogs mixed in with them. In the distance down the road, he thought he heard a car door shut. The house was still. A few lights on the main floor were still on, but he couldn't see anyone inside. He stared into those windows, but nothing. Then a moment later he took the bottle of whiskey and took another long pull. Then a minute after, he took another. And then another. He felt the apparent heaviness to his head, though his mind was now lighter and he was lost somewhere in the contradiction.

A light flicked off, and then another. Now the house was black inside. After a half hour he quietly cracked open the car door and slid outside. He walked over to the tall grass on the side of the road where the crickets sang and took a long piss. The insects scattered and the whole time he thought about how much noise he was making. He decided he didn't care and when he was done he zipped up and returned to his car. He sat back down in the driver's seat and leaned his head back. The fuzzy cloth on the seat never felt more comfortable on the back of his head.

A light flicked on. It was to an upstairs room and Mason suddenly snapped his head forward and watched. At first there was still no movement. But then a girl stepped into view. It was her. She had a towel around her body and a towel wrapped over her head. She stood in front of the open window and didn't move for a few moments. Mason watched her. The fog rose slightly, or maybe he imagined it, and then he thought he was surely living a dream—or a nightmare. The look on the girl's face was calm. She stared out the window and Mason knew she must be staring at him. She knew he was there. It was haunting. With the towel on her head covering her hair, the beauty of her face was heightened. It was her. Chloe.

Mason thought about stepping back out of the car. Throwing rocks at the window with force, until it broke, and shouting that he was sorry but for her to go away, that he'd been punished enough and he'd never live a day without the burden and regret of that night. He wanted to apologize for the pain he caused her—and her family. Why was she appearing now? What was the significance? Was six years the limit—survive that long and it becomes time to relive the pain. Would this become a ritual?

"You're not real," he heard himself whisper softly under his breath. It didn't even feel like the words came from his own mouth. He listened intently to himself.

"Go away. Disappear. You're not really there."

He took another swig from the bottle and this time it didn't go down so smoothly and he felt a burn on his tongue and down his throat and all the way into his stomach and he coughed through closed lips.

"Get out of my head."

She kept staring. The night was so dark and she was so bright in that window. Her skin was so gentle and perfect. She was so innocent.

"Get out of my head."

He took another drink and this time welcomed the pain.

"God, why. Why did you let me do this?"

He took another drink.

"I came to this fuckin place to run away from this."

Another drink.

"Why are you doing this to me? Damn it. God. Please. Why."

Another drink.

He wanted to cry. He felt his breathing quicken and his chest was tight and he winced. The muscles in his cheeks flexed with all his strength and he tried to force the tears but they wouldn't come. Maybe he wasn't as remorseful as he hoped he would be. He took another drink. He tipped the bottle all the way back and the last drop fell onto his tongue and disappeared.

Out of the corner of his eye he saw something and when he looked back up to the window the light was off. She was gone and he thanked God for listening and then he leaned back and fell asleep.

10

The whiskey bottle was still tucked under his arm. Mason rolled his head from left to right and slowly opened his eyes. He was still lost somewhere very far away, a place where he could never return. And then he allowed his vision to gradually adjust and when it did, he realized he was still in his car parked outside of the house. The sun was out.

A neighbor was jogging by and Mason quickly hid the bottle under a jacket in the backseat. He glanced in the rearview mirror—he looked like shit. His eyes were bloodshot, his hair sweaty and messy. There was something poking into his lower back and he arched forward and pulled out his hat from behind him. It was a little deformed—it must have fallen off while he slept—but he punched it back out to the best form he could and put it on. He looked into the mirror again. Still looked like shit, but better. It was certainly the best he could do.

For a short instant he thought he could drive home and change, but the sun's height tipped him off to the time of day and he looked at the clock. It was already after eight—Terry and the other two men would be arriving soon. He had no other options. He would have to stay.

A pair of ravens landed on an overhanging branch near his window and he watched them for a few moments while he tried to recover. They peered around the area and then froze for a moment, as if listening. Then they peered some more and took off in flight for another branch further down the road to where Mason could barely see them. They were fascinating to him. He was always envious of the birds, being able to fly freely whenever they wanted—and the larger birds, well more power to them. He thought about what it would be like to fly away and he leaned back and closed his eyes for a second, and when he opened them the two other workers were standing outside his door staring at him.

"Look at you," the first one said.

And then finishing his friend's sentence, the second said, "Just sleepin in the car."

Mason jolted himself fully awake and opened the car door and started to climb out, then ducked back in to pull the keys from the ignition. Thankfully he had shut off the engine the night before. He greeted the two men as casually as he could and shook their hands. "Boys," he said.

"You never beat us here."

"Yeah, what—you sleep here last night er something?"

Mason quickly deflected the question. "Nah. So what's goin on, guys?" He must have begun to seem flustered.

They looked at him curiously. "You good, man?" one said.

"Yeah, I'm good."

"Good."

The three walked up the drive and into the backyard and they stopped to look at the lake. The sun to their right was high enough in the sky to create a shiny glare over the surface and they had to squint when they looked at it. One of the men held up his arm across his forehead to shield the brightness.

"God damn gorgeous," the man said.

His buddy nodded.

The man glanced back at the house, then back to the water. "Hard to believe anyone has this kinda cash. I could save every dollar I make the rest of my life and never afford a place like this."

His buddy's nod became more exaggerated.

"You could do it," Mason said.

"How's that?"

He really didn't know, he just felt like being encouraging. "I don't know. But you never know. Get an idea, it takes off."

"Right."

Mason doubted men like this would ever make anything of

themselves, but then he thought neither would he. He could have, the way he was raised, he probably could have had a life of luxury handed to him. Hell, he was already living a life of luxury when he walked out—if luxury, of course, is measured in material possessions.

"You got any ideas?" the man asked Mason.

"Not right now."

"The problem is," the second man chimed in. "It's hard to get anything going in an economy like this."

"Oh, so you got an idea to get rich?" the first asked.

"That's not what I'm sayin. Just sayin, it ain't gonna happen in Marquette, Michigan. That's fer sure."

"Makes sense."

Then Mason said, "I like it here."

The other two men laughed. "Right. You just show up in this town a few years ago and you actually like it?"

He nodded. "Mhmm."

"What's yer deal, anyway? No one just moves to this place."

"I got nowhere else to be, so I figured I'd give this place a try and I've liked it so far."

"Shit, man," the first man said. "Like I said before, I'd take my ass to California or someplace warm if I was you."

"I have no interest in California," Mason said. The truth was, Mason had thought about moving out West. It would get him nearly as far from the accident as possible without leaving the country. There was so much land, so much forest to trek into and disappear. But then he thought he'd already found enough of that in the UP. That is, until his sins decided to revisit him. And that's when he realized it didn't matter where he wandered—they would follow him anywhere he went.

"That's a good call," the second man said. "Bunch of weirdos on the West Coast."

"That's right," said the first man.

"Alright," Mason said, changing the subject. "So what do we have left to do here?"

"Just finish her up," a voice said, and the three of them turned to see Terry walking up behind them. "Morning, boys."

"Sir," Mason said as a greeting.

Terry dropped his hand onto Mason's shoulder and then gave him a little squeeze. "It looks good, boys. Finish her up over there," he said, pointing. "And then we should be good." He paused and joined the three men looking out at the lake. "Gonna miss working this damn place."

"I hear ya."

"Definitely."

"Yup."

Terry spit into the lawn and then patted one of the other men on the back. "That's why we do a hell of a job, so they call us back." He looked around the lawn again nodding and then said, "I gotta jet to another job. Call me when you boys are done here."

As Terry walked toward the driveway a man stepped out

the back door, waved to the three men and then he and Terry began talking. It seemed to go peacefully and a few minutes later they shook hands and Terry gave his workers a look and then continued down the driveway. The man waved again and then walked inside. Mason and the other two each went back to work, putting on the finishing touches to the lawn and the patio area.

They were working hard for a couple of hours and as the sun reached its peak the air felt hot and humid and the occasional breeze off the lake was as refreshing as a cold glass of water. Mason's hands were covered in thick black dirt and he nudged his cap higher over his forehead with the back of his arm and then wiped the sweat away. His hair was tangled and sticking to the sides of his head and his neck. Now would be a great time to shave it all off, he thought.

He was just about to get back to work when he heard one of the other men say in a quiet voice, "Damn." Mason didn't think anything of it until the man then said, "*That* must be the girl you were askin about."

Mason looked up. There she was. She was wearing a backward hat, a purple bikini top and tight khaki shorts. She was carrying a small stack of cups in one hand and a pitcher in the other. Her eyes were locked on Mason and his were locked on her. The other men were staring too—they saw her. She was real. Mason's heart was racing as she walked closer. She couldn't be real. This couldn't be happening. He felt his head get lighter and his face got hot and he nearly passed out.

"Chill, man," one of the men said, nudging him.

The girl stopped in front of him and Mason continued staring at her. He kept envisioning the newspaper article. You're not here, he told himself.

"I have some lemonade for you guys," she said. She smiled. Her voice was as sweet and innocent as she looked. She handed the cups over to one of the other men and then passed off the pitcher.

"Thanks," they each said. They started pouring glasses for themselves and downing nearly half in one drink.

The girl turned to Mason. He was still frozen and must have had a look of terror on his face. She stuck out her hand. "Mallory," she said.

He flinched. "No," he instinctively reacted.

She looked confused.

Finally he held up his hands to show the amount of dirt. "Sorry. My name's Mason. I'm sorry, your name is...?"

"Mallory," she said again.

"Mallory," he repeated to himself. "Sorry, you looked like someone—" He cut himself off and thought for a second.

"I get that a lot," she said and smiled again. She looked a little nervous herself, but she didn't walk away. "You ran off so quickly the other day." Now she had her hands on the front of her shorts with her thumbs tucked underneath.

"Yeah, sorry about that." It couldn't be her. She said her name was Mallory. She said she gets that a lot—a familiar face. Calm yourself. Breathe.

"You apologize too much," she said with a teasing look.

"Yeah."

"My folks just bought this place."

"It's an amazing house."

She nodded. "It is. I've never even been to the UP before."

"Oh, it's a great place." Mason glanced over at the other two men. They were drinking their lemonade and watching the girl intently. "These clowns don't think so. I always have, though." He nodded toward his coworkers.

"How long have you lived here?"

"About six years."

"That's a while." She looked at the water, and then back to Mason. "So, Mason. You think you could show me around maybe? I'd like to see the area." She rocked forward and backward, ever so slightly, from her heels to her toes.

For a moment he thought. And then he said, "I could probably do that."

"Great," she said with genuine enthusiasm.

"Tonight work for you?"

She smiled and nodded.

"We should be done here in an hour or so. I could get you around eight, if that works?"

"Perfect." She took a step backward and then looked back over to the other two. "How's the lemonade?"

"Good."

"Great."

"I'm glad," she said as she headed back to the house. Mason

and the other two watched her all the way inside. She seemed to have a new energy in her walk.

When she disappeared into the house one of the men looked at Mason. "You son of a bitch," he said.

Mason looked over at the man, who was cracking a smirk. Mason just smiled.

"How the hell did you just do that?"

He thought for a moment and looked back into the house. "I guess things are looking up for me."

11

Mason spent the remainder of the afternoon thinking about Mallory, about how much she looked like Chloe, about how they couldn't be the same person and about how crazy he had allowed himself to become.

She has a familiar face, he told himself, she had said it herself. That wasn't her. And thank God that it wasn't. You're not crazy—that's what this means. Take a deep breath and get back to that place you were before this girl came to town. The complacent place where you spent evenings in the woods, where you never thought of a life outside the vast northern wilderness, where nothing was great but where you could live with your sins. For a few days she had taken that contentment from you, but now it's coming back.

Mason was driving home now and he thought about what that contentment really meant. He thought about how sad a life it was. How there were people out there busting their asses to make something of this life God had given them, and about how he was throwing his away. But then he thought, it wasn't your choice to throw it away. These sins, this life—it was thrust upon you and you had no choice in the matter. You didn't have to drink, the good side of his conscience reminded him. But then the level side stepped back in and told him it was okay, that there was nothing wrong with living a simple life. And then—it wasn't just a simple life, it was a cowardly life in which you'd rather ignore the truth than face it. You need to calm down.

He pulled through the woods and back to his cabin and his head was spinning. There was Jones, sitting in the same chair in which he sat every single day. Jones nodded toward the young man but otherwise sat motionless in his chair. It wasn't until Mason stepped out of the car and walked toward his cabin that Jones began rocking.

"Good day?" the old man asked.

Mason didn't know how to respond. Yes and no. "Not bad," he finally said.

"Good." Jones continued rocking and Mason walked into the cabin. He thought about that old man, about everything he'd been through in life, and about the choices he'd made to land him where he sat. That was a man who had made mistakes, sure, but then he punished himself. He made the decision to move into the woods and he made the decision to stay in the woods. Mason was on his way to doing the same thing. He could see himself in forty or fifty years sitting in that same chair on that same porch, rocking gently while the evening sun glared over the pasture before him. But was it really the life he deserved? He just couldn't convince himself it wasn't. And until that day, he would continue living it.

Once inside, Mason's mind rather quickly turned back to Mallory. He thought about how beautiful she looked in the afternoon, about their conversation. It still didn't feel real to him. It felt like he'd lived a dream, a foggy, light-headed moment that would come and go through his mind when it was most convenient—and more likely inconvenient.

Mason stripped down and stepped into the shower and let the warm water wash over him. He closed his eyes and aimed his face directly at the faucet. It felt nice, refreshing. He wanted to continue standing there all day and block everything else in the world from his mind. There was the constant rush of water acting as white noise. He continued just standing there. Then after a few minutes he began what he was there to do, and picked up the bar of soap.

When he was done showering, he covered himself with a towel and walked into his bedroom. The pasture where the cabin sat was surrounded by steep hills and overshadowing trees, which did well to keep the sun from beaming directly onto the roof all day, but which also did well to keep the heat from escaping. Mason slid open a window in his room and he immediately felt the cool rush of a summer breeze enter, so he walked down the hallway into the living room and opened two more windows. The cabin cooled quickly and he breathed deeply and sat down, still only in his towel, and aimed a box fan into his face to keep himself from sweating before he got dressed. He made only subtle movements, trying to use as little energy as possible to hold off the perspiration.

Now all he could think about was Mallory. For the first time in six years, he cared about what he would wear. He thought about what he had in his closet—very little, so his options would be scarce. When he knew he was cooled off and comfortable, he stood once more and walked back into the bathroom. He stood in front of the mirror and dropped his towel. He looked at himself closely. He had never taken the time to notice that over the last six years, he had become a stranger to himself entirely. He didn't recognize the person standing before him. The look in his eyes was lifeless and he stared back trying to remember who he had once been.

Then he thought, this is good. This is a new girl. This is a new start. Maybe God is beginning to forgive you. Maybe He is telling you that you need to begin to forgive yourself and get on with your life. It's your chance to start new. This is not your sins haunting you, it's God telling you that it's okay to move on. The ultimate forgiveness.

For a moment he weighed the possibility that it was true.

But quickly he disregarded its meaning and went back into his room and threw on a faded polo and a pair of jeans that he'd bought at a thrift store a couple years before. On the floor there were three pairs of boots—that was really all he ever wore these days. Two of the pairs were scuffed with lines and had worn edges from all the landscaping and hiking through the woods, but the third pair—brown and rounded at the toe—were still in relatively good shape and he pulled them on and then tucked the legs of his jeans over the top. He added a hat and walked back to look in the mirror. It'll do, he thought, and then put on deodorant and walked back out the front door.

The old man was still sitting in the same wooden rocking chair on the porch and he only moved his head to watch Mason. Mason nodded as he started toward his car.

"Dinner?" Jones said.

"Can't tonight."

"Where ya headed?"

"Got a date," Mason said reluctantly.

The old man smiled. "Well I'll be damned."

"Don't get too excited. I'm just showing a girl around town who's never been here before, is all."

"Right," Jones said. "Don't go spendin too much on her though, you still owe me rent."

"I haven't gotten that to you yet?"

"Ain't seen a dime."

"Sorry about that. I'll get it to you tomorrow."

The old man rocked a little and then said, "I been remindin you an awful lot recently."

"I know, I'll get it to you."

"Just don't want ya thinkin you can pay me whenever's good fer ya. There's a schedule I gotta keep around here."

"It won't be late again," Mason said.

"The hell it won't," Jones said, and then seemingly to himself added, "Some folks just don't change."

Mason heard it clearly and thought about that comment as he climbed into his car and started off down the road. For whatever reason it got to him.

Those words echoed in his head just like the traumas of his past. Mason cruised down the two-lane road and tried to shake the old man's statement. It didn't matter what he said, he thought. That's just one man's opinion. What mattered was the girl who was about to climb into the car. He pictured her face—a face he knew so well, if only from its familiarity. Regardless of who it really belonged to, it would continue to illicit the nightmares of Mason's past. It was still too real—and yet, he refused to believe that it happened. If only he could live an isolated life of solitude and refrain from negatively impacting the lives of others, then maybe it could be erased from all existence.

His mind was going this way, thoughts zigzagging and slashing their way through his mind until he found himself pulling onto Mallory's street. It was a calm evening and as he headed west the sun, just barely peeking over the tree line, met his eyes with a blinding force. He squinted and moved his face around to try to avoid the glare until he eased his car to a stop in front of her home.

Mason waited for a moment before proceeding. He took a deep breath and stared at the house. What are you getting yourself into, he thought. This is too much. This is certainly not solitude. After a few moments he glanced up again and saw the front door open. An older man stood motionless in the doorway and looked outward. He appeared to look over to Mason but then he turned and looked up the street. A moment later his attention was turned to something beside him in the house. That was when Mallory appeared and hugged him. He embraced her and kissed the top of her head. They exchanged a word and Mallory smiled and then ran out the door toward Mason's car. He stepped out and stood next to the car to wait for her to walk up, and then he went to her side of the car and greeted her. His stomach churned with nerves. Over her shoulder Mason could see her father nod and then close himself back in the house. Mason's gaze returned to Mallory. She was now approaching, her hair light and lifting in the light breeze with each step. She was stunning.

"Hi," he said. His hands briefly formed loose fists and he could feel the slippery sweat forming.

"Thanks for getting me," she said, and then she smiled that damn smile that haunted his dreams and nightmares.

Before reaching for the door, he quickly wiped the sweat on his jeans and then opened the car for her.

"Very polite of you."

"No problem." He wanted to hug her but then he thought it was probably better that he didn't, so he closed the door behind her and hurried back around to his side and climbed inside.

He did his best to keep his cool but his heart rate was intensifying, so he tried to take deep breaths to calm himself. He glanced over at Mallory and she was even more beautiful than he even previously thought. She looked over at him and smiled, and then she looked out the window and asked, "So where are you taking me?"

He couldn't think of an answer. Truly he didn't know. But when she asked him to show her around, he couldn't refuse. It may have been the look in her eye, or the urge to prove to himself that he could feel again—or even that he deserved to feel again. They were driving down a two-lane road that wound and curved as it ascended, and then it slowly rolled downward and they stayed along it until they came into town. First they just cruised the streets and he tried to point out small landmarks that he knew, and she would look onward and nod as he spoke. He could tell she wasn't into his tour, but he continued to give it nonetheless. After about twenty minutes they came to a stoplight and Mason looked at her and asked, "So what do you think?"

"I think it's a neat town," she said. Her window was rolled down and the cool evening air of summer floated into the car. "What do you think?"

"I agree," he said. "Pretty neat town."

Then she said, "Let's keep driving," and so Mason drove.

Eventually he decided to stop driving down the same city blocks and took a right-hand turn and headed back out into the country.

"Now where are we going?"

"I'm not sure," he said honestly.

"Can we get something to drink?" she asked.

He was caught a little off-guard by the request. "What were you thinking?"

"I want rum and Coke." She had an innocent smile that Mason couldn't resist and at the first store he passed that sold liquor he parked the car and ran inside. A minute later he returned and handed Mallory a brown paper bag.

"Thanks!" She smiled again and clutched the back tightly and then leaned her face out the window as they pulled back onto the road.

The sun wasn't gone but it was now tucked behind the trees and Mason drove until he found a place to park high on a hill outside of town. There was a vast forest below them and out into the distance they could see the lake that extended to the infinite horizon.

"Will this do?" he asked.

"Perfect."

She reached inside the bag and pulled out a bottle of Captain Morgan, a two liter of Coke and a small stack of plastic party cups.

"No ice?" she asked.

Shit, he thought. But then he glanced back up at her and she was smiling again.

"Just kidding," she said and organized the liquids to pour them drinks. "How much do you want?"

"Whatever you're having."

"Okay." Mallory unscrewed the lids and filled two cups with a strong mixture of rum and Coke, and then she handed one over to Mason. "Cheers," she said. They clinked the cups together and each took a sip. Mallory winced and then held the back of her hand over her mouth and coughed. "Whoa, stronger than I thought."

Mason smiled and took a second sip. It went down too smooth for him. He looked over at Mallory. Her eyes watered slightly and she tried to smile back.

Then Mallory turned in her seat to face Mason and said, "So tell me about yourself."

"What do you want to know?"

"Just tell me something. How old are you?"

"Twenty-five. What about you?"

"I just turned nineteen," she said. And then she asked, "Where are you from?"

Mason set his cup down, then lifted his cap off his head and brushed his hair back, and then replaced the hat. Without looking over at her, he plainly said "Chicago" as he stared out the front windshield at the forest. When he finally looked over at her she was smiling with clear eyes and she lifted her eyebrows as if waiting for him to continue. All he could think about now was his hometown. It had been a long time since he thought about that place and that life.

"When did you move here?"

"About six years ago," he said.

"Oh," she said softly. For a brief moment she mellowed, but she rebounded quickly and perked back up. She took another sip, and now the booze slid down her throat without a burn. "So you like it up here?"

"Yeah it's not bad. It's quiet and things move pretty slow but I like that."

"They definitely move slower," she said and offered a quick laugh.

There was silence for a minute and they held their cups and the windows were rolled down and the night air seeped into the car. Mason's heart was racing. He tried to calm himself. This girl was amazing. Her charm was overwhelming him and he tried to keep a level head. "Your turn," he said. "Tell me a little about yourself."

She gave a teasing look and asked, "What do you want to know?" She tucked her feet underneath herself and was still facing Mason.

He couldn't help but smile. "Anything," he said. "Tell me about your family or where you grew up."

She took another sip and her head tilted all the way back and she emptied her cup. "Not right now," she said politely with a smile and then took her cup and Mason's and poured new drinks. When she handed it back to him they bumped them together and drank. Then she set her cup down and took his back from him and set it next to hers and without hesitation climbed over onto Mason's seat and started kissing him. For a moment he was stunned but went along with it and wrapped his arms around her and she was moving her hands up and down his torso and they continued kissing. He fell backward onto the seat and reached down and reclined it quickly and they collapsed with it. They each braced themselves for the drop but then continued kissing. Mason ran his hands underneath Mallory's shirt and she tugged his upward until she got it over his head. Mason couldn't believe this was happening. It was all going so fast. It had been a long time since he'd even kissed a girl. Now this.

As lightly as he could, he slid her shirt upward but was apparently not working fast enough and she finished the job for him, and then they returned their lips together. They kissed for a few more minutes, moving their heads side to side, and Mallory unclasped her bra and Mason felt her warm skin on his chest. Then Mallory pulled her head back and smiled at him. He returned the look. Then she rolled onto the passenger's seat and held her feet in the air and she slid her pants off. For a moment Mason watched her but then thought it would be best if his were off by the time she climbed back on top of him, and so he did the same. When she mounted him a warm sensation ran through his body and their lips pressed back together for a long time and they never parted, even when the breathing intensified, until they were finished and she pulled back again and smiled at him and slowly crawled back to the other seat.

They each lay there just breathing for a minute. The cool evening air was rolling in and slowly forcing their steam out of the car. Mason stuck his head out the window and filled his lungs with the fresh air and then plopped back down in the seat. He glanced over at her. She was still naked and sat limp in the seat. No rush for getting dressed. When she looked back at him she had innocence in her eyes and he smiled. He was happy. It was a feeling he hadn't felt in some time. True happiness.

Mallory gathered her clothes and started to put them back on. Mason opened his door and swung his feet outside. His jeans were still around his ankles caught over his boots, so he pulled them back up and then stood and slipped his shirt over his head. Mallory followed his lead and stepped out of her door too and they looked at each other from over the car once they were fully dressed again. Then a moment later she broke out laughing and Mason couldn't help but smile.

"That was unexpected," he finally said.

"Yes it was," she agreed. "Another drink?"

He nodded and then turned and looked out over the woods as she poured the rum and then walked around the car and handed it to him. "Thanks."

"No problem."

He took a sip. "I've got to be honest with you," he started.

"That was my first time in a while."

"You wouldn't know it. You were good." She shot him a wink.

He laughed and took another sip. "I didn't have to do anything, so I think I have to thank you for doing all the work."

She took a curtsy and said, "The pleasure was mine."

"Let's sit back down," Mason said. "My legs are like Jell-O right now."

"Let's sit on the hood. We need to let the car air out a little."

"Fine by me."

Mallory hopped up on top of the car's hood and Mason carefully slid next to her, knowing his weight would put a dent in it if he gave it any momentum. They pressed their backs against the windshield and stretched out their legs. Above them, the night sky was black and millions of bright stars appeared. The moon was nearly full out over the lake in the distance, casting light with its star companions that shed over the tops of the trees well enough that Mason could see clearly where the lake ended and the forest began. The crickets chirped in the brush and the nighttime bugs sang their songs in the trees. The occasional breeze blew past and it cooled their skin and then sent a ruffle into the woods. A light-headed buzz softened Mason's feelings and he thought for the first time in a long time that he was content with life.

The calm silence was finally broken when Mallory began speaking. "Thanks for bringing me out here," she said quietly, as if not to disturb the scene.

"I'm glad you came. I spend a lot of time out in these woods by myself, it's nice to have company."

"You sit out here by yourself?"

"Well I don't come all the way out here, really, but I built sort of a tree house in the woods near where I live and I go out there alone quite a bit."

"I spent a lot of time by myself too," Mallory admitted. "Not out in places like this. Usually it's just in my room or around the house or whatever."

"An outgoing girl like you? That surprises me."

"Outgoing?" she asked as if questioning his assessment.

"You didn't even know me, yet you asked me to take you around the area. That's pretty outgoing in my book."

"I guess you're right." She took another sip. "I don't think it's that I'm outgoing, really. When we were talking earlier I just felt like I knew you, that's all."

"Is that right?"

"Yeah. I don't know."

They stopped talking for another minute.

Then, without any provocation, she just said it. "When I was thirteen, my sister was killed."

Mason froze. He lost feeling in his face and his arms and his legs, and he could feel his heart beating out of his chest but he couldn't feel his chest. He could feel the blood pumping through his face.

Mallory must have seen the terror on his face, because then she said, "I'm sorry. I know, too personal."

"What happened?" Mason said plainly. He couldn't feel the words coming off of his tongue.

"She was nineteen..."

Like a knife to the gut.

"...and we were on vacation near Ludington..."

His throat was tightening.

"...and she and my mom got in a huge fight..."

Rapid breathing. Chest tightening.

"...so she went for a late night walk to get out of the house..."

A rush of nausea.

"...and someone hit her with their car."

He could feel the vomit in the back of his throat. He held his hand to his chest and tried to suppress the beating. "Oh my God."

Mallory didn't flinch. The story didn't seem to faze her, like she'd told it too many times before. "It was the worst day of my life," she said. And then, "They never even caught the person who did it. The bastard just drove off." The look on her face began to soften and she finished by saying, "And the worst part was that we didn't find her for a couple hours, and the doctor told us that she could have been saved if she would have been found a little sooner."

He said "Oh my God" again, but he was thinking, "It was me! I did it! I killed her! I'm a murderer!" He had no idea the girl was still alive, that all he had to do was stay to help her, an indefinite incarceration but maybe a life saved and a conscience cleared. That realization only added to the weight of his guilt.

"My sister was an amazing person. Losing her is the reason I feel like such a loner, like some kind of purpose was taken from my life. And then I met you and, I don't know, I just felt a connection, you know?"

"I know," he said softly, but he was thinking about his confession, about spending eternity in hell. About how he would face the Lord and pay for his sins. About how he would confront the truth. About how he would give this innocent girl closure on her pain from the past.

"That's actually why we moved up here. We had the place near Ludington my whole life, but my parents just couldn't take going there anymore so we sold it and got the place here."

Mason tried to listen to what she was saying but the voices in his head were deafening.

When Mason didn't respond, she said, "Sorry for all the personal information." She tried to brush it off with a forced smirk and then took another drink to empty her cup.

You have to tell her, he thought. Is it better to confess your sin or live with the guilt of getting away with it? Regardless, you're going to have to answer to God eventually.

Mallory leaned over and tried to rest her head on Mason's shoulder but he flinched and sat up and slid off the hood and landed on his feet. He couldn't feel the ground beneath him and had to keep his balance by holding onto the car.

"What's wrong?" she asked.

Now's not the time to tell her, he told himself. Now's not the time. Now's not the time. He was losing his mind.

"I'm sorry," she said.

"I'm sorry," Mason repeated. And then he said, "I'm sorry, but we have to go."

12

Of course he should have known. He'd read the article a thousand times. He knew there was a sister. What the hell was he thinking? But her name wasn't Mallory in the article. Middle name? Can't put two and two together? He blinded himself and now what was he going to do?

The roads out of the woods and back through town and up toward Mallory's house seemed to narrow and twist with more difficulty than Mason remembered the first time around. His sight seemed to vibrate with the rapid beating of his chest. The radio was on but he couldn't hear it. He could only hear his thoughts running through his head telling him he was going to hell. To calm down. To lose your mind. To panic. To breathe. And then he looked at Mallory and she seemed upset and confused and she didn't say a word the entire drive back.

As they neared her house, Mason found it somewhere within himself to take a few deep breaths and slow the car to a normal pace. They cruised up to her house and he put it in park, but left it running. When he turned to her, he could see she'd been crying, at least a few tears. He owed it to her, for all he had done, to leave her with the best impression he could.

"I'm sorry about all that," he said.

She looked at him and sniffled for a breath and then composed herself. "What happened?"

"I just—there's this old man," he said as he thought how to continue the sentence. Finally he said, "I rent my cabin from him. I forgot I was supposed to pick a few things up for him. He's sick." Lying seemed the least of his worries at this point. He was living one great one, after all.

"Ah."

"Look, I really am sorry." Just tell her, he thought. No, that would be stupid. "I had a great time tonight. Better than I deserved."

"Are you sure you're okay?"

"I'll be okay."

"Okay. Well I had a good time too. Thanks for showing me around." She leaned over and gave Mason a kiss on the cheek and his body ran cold when her lips connected. Then she climbed out of the car and through the open window asked,

"Can I see you again?"

For a moment he thought, "Not likely." But to her he said, "Yes." He jotted down his number and handed it to her. She slid it into her pocket and forced a smile and left. When she was back in the house he reached into his pocket for his phone, held down the power button and turned it off. Then he drove, scared and distraught, back to his cabin.

Clouds had begun to roll in and the cool air was now heavier with moisture. The stars slowly began to disappear behind the thick charcoal sky. By the time he reached the narrow road that led back to the field where his cabin sat, a sprinkle of rain had begun falling. His headlights were on bright and they cut across the old man's cabin before he stopped the car and they aimed for a quick second into the woods. Mason caught a glimpse of a light illuminating inside the old man's cabin but he didn't pay it any mind and headed straight into his own. It only took him a few minutes—he packed some clothes, some books, the Bible, a few toiletries—before he was ready to head back outside.

Now the rain was real. It was coming down at a steady pace and Mason braced himself as he carried two full duffle bags to his car and hurled them into the back seat. When he started to pull out, he saw the old man step out onto his porch. Mason thought he saw him hold up a hand, as if to stop the boy, but he continued driving. His only thought was to get away. He had to leave. Now. Maybe he would return, maybe not. That was a decision for later. The thoughts in his head never shut off. You're a coward, he told himself. You run away from your problems. You don't face your fears or the consequences or even the truth. You run and you'll always run because you're a runner.

Down the road he was driving with his windshield wipers speeding back and forth to fight the onslaught of rain. He blinked and tried to clear the buzz from his head. He said a quick prayer that he could focus—though he didn't expect anyone to listen. He was driving westward and when he got out of town the road curved and sliced through the forests, sloping downward and then climbing and then falling back downward. He drove for nearly two hours into the dense forest and then he pulled off the main road onto a dirt path that was barely wide enough for his car. He bounced and shifted as the holes and ruts in the road had their way with the small vehicle. Eventually he came out into a small clearing and checked the gas gauge and he was nearing empty, so he turned off the car and grabbed his bags and climbed out. The sun was just beginning to shine new light on the woods and the rain had moved out and the humidity set in and Mason smacked mosquitoes on his arms and neck as he walked into the woods.

He had no direction, no sense of place or location or even reason for wandering but he continued nonetheless. The land where he had lived was now cursed. His sins followed him there and he had to escape. Escape or perish—that was his mindset. But he knew he could only run for so long, so far until the running would stop and he would begin his death sentence.

On his right in the thick of the woods was a large pine tree, its lowest branches about five feet off the ground, and he ducked beneath it and took a seat against the trunk. He sat there silently and listened to the noises of the forest and tried to calm himself. Finally, he felt he'd given himself some type of freedom—undeserved, but freedom nonetheless. He closed his eyes and put his head back and looked up the tree at the branches. He thought about climbing to the top, but thought better of it. Then he closed his eyes again and this time he saw the girl's face. Her name was Chloe. She had a name. She had so much to live for. And you took it all away from her. And she has a sister, and her name is Mallory, and you just—holy shit. He thought about what they'd done a few hours earlier. What he had done with the sister of the girl he killed. Just piling on the sins. They will follow him forever. Eternity. Which he will spend in hell.

These were the thoughts going through Mason's head as he finally began to drift away. He fell asleep sitting against the tree and then a little while later he awoke from the gentle sound of a nearby twig breaking. His eyes shot open and he stood and a little ways down the path was a cougar. It was standing facing Mason and it was still and its eyes didn't move. Mason froze. He didn't know what to do. He squinted and looked at the beast closely and he thought to himself, could this be the same cougar that he'd seen a few days before? But it was so far from where he'd last seen it. But it had been forced from its territory by the wolves. And now it lived here. And now it was face-to-face with Mason, who was invading its land. There was going to be a winner and there was going to be a loser. And only the winner may claim the land, and the loser will be back off to Nod.

Book II:

The Hills of Mercy

1

There was a certain way about her, Davey couldn't explain it. Like she had some type of secret that only she knew, and the rest of the world merely had to watch from afar as she giggled to herself, because knowing this secret led to a modest yet powerful life and she couldn't comprehend its value nor why only she was privy to it. It wasn't an arrogance. Davey thought that maybe it was that she knew exactly who she was and where she stood, and really it was just an understanding or an acceptance that most people never reach. Regardless, it didn't seem too important to him. He was a sixteen-year-old boy and he was content with just looking at her.

Claire was sitting on a fallen tree trunk that poked out over the running creek below just far enough so that she could dangle her toes in the water and fish. Davey stood beside her in the grass and cast from the shore. It was late in the afternoon and evening was approaching quickly, though there was still plenty of sun to work with. In fact, the sun was in a perfect position in the sky to play on Claire. Davey loved fishing with her, but not because she was good company—in fact, she kept quiet much of the time—and not because she was an excellent angler. No, it was because she was beautiful and any excuse for him to stare at her next to the riverbank for a few hours was good enough for him.

Davey was an awkward kid, to put it mildly. He had shaggy brown hair that wouldn't lie down, a boney frame and summertime freckles that seemed to keep the girls away. All the girls except Claire, that is. Maybe it was because they were more or less neighbors and had known each other longer than any other kids in school. Davey didn't like to think of it that way. He liked to pretend they just understood one another, that when they isolated themselves from their other friends life simply made more senoo. Whatever the reason, it was working for him.

Claire was still sitting on the log and turned her head to look at Davey, who had an absent stare fixated on her. She must have been used to these looks from all the boys and smiled and watched the water puttering past. As tough as she was, Claire was a petite girl, and short, and at fifteen the only evidence she was becoming a woman came from her slightly maturing waistline. Her hair was dark brown, but in the right light would shimmer with a hint of red. The skin on her face was smooth and flawless and fair, which she attributed to the climate in Michigan's Upper Peninsula. That's what she always assumed drew the boys to her—a complexion which would seem to yield a dark skin tone, yet was uniquely pale. She used it to her advantage. She could play the innocent, gentle girl, or she could pierce with an icy look that was also uniquely Claire.

When she turned back to him, Davey was still staring and this time pretended to be looking off into the distance at the water and the trees. She laughed.

"Can I help you?" she asked playfully.

He protruded his lower lip and shook his head. "Nah, just looking around."

"Smooth," she said, and then she reeled in her line and spun around and climbed back to shore. She walked over beside Davey and cast from the shore. She was doing her best to make him nervous and they fished in silence for a little while longer, until Claire finally reeled in the line for the final time and said that she needed to take off.

"What do you have going on?" Davey asked.

"I'm supposed to meet up with Russell."

"Ah," he said, nodding as nonchalantly as he could in an attempt to hide his displeasure.

"Cheer up."

With that she headed back from the creek and Davey followed. They cut down a dirt path that had been worn from years of teenagers sneaking down it late at night. It was only a couple feet wide, with high grass and weeds lining it on both sides so that it tickled your arms when you walked by and you had to carry your fishing pole across your shoulders to avoid it getting caught. That's how Davey and Claire walked, with Claire taking the lead. That was fine with Davey, he never minded having to follow her. The path curved gradually and they were careful not to trip on thick roots that bulged from the flattened dirt beneath their feet. After a couple minutes they emerged on the side of a dirt road and picked up their bikes that were leaning against a nearby tree, tucked just out of sight from any passing cars—though passersby were very few and far between. They would have preferred to drive, but Davey's older brother had borrowed his truck and wouldn't be home until late.

A minute later on their bikes they were riding side-by-side, slowly down the road with their poles in one hand and the other loosely gripping the handlebar. By this time the sun was beginning to disappear over the trees and in the forest nighttime approaches much quicker than in the city.

"Getting dark in a hurry," Davey noted.

"Yeah it is."

They continued riding and the road eventually turned to pavement and then a little while later they came to Davey's house. He veered up his driveway and felt a quick pinch of anxiety in his stomach when he watched her continue riding.

"See ya later," he called, but he wasn't sure if she heard him. He rode slowly until he stopped completely and watched her fade away as she distanced herself from him, and when she was gone altogether he turned up his driveway and tried to put her out of his mind—never an easy task.

—   —   —

Claire, on the other hand, picked up speed as she rode down the street. She was excited and made a right on the next road and pedaled quickly until she felt the burn in her quads. It was difficult using only one hand and eventually she managed to grip the handlebars with two hands and pin the fishing rod beneath her right.

When she made it home she changed out of her tank top and jeans and slid into a cotton summer dress that was light green with horizontal white stripes and was nearly thin enough to see through. She stood in front of the full-length mirror and looked at herself. With both hands, she funneled her hair behind her head and then held it there to see how she would look with it pulled back. A moment later she let it fall back over her shoulders and she shook it out, running her fingertips through it. Good enough, she thought.

She grabbed her phone off her dresser and checked it. There were a couple short messages from Russell and she read them through and then gave him a call.

After a few rings he said, "Hey you."

"Where are you?" she asked.

"Almost there, almost there."

"Well geez, hurry."

"Two minutes."

He hung up and she put her phone in a small clutch and slid the strap over her left wrist. Her mother was still at work and she walked outside and sat down on the wicker chair on the porch. It was a clear night now and the stars were brightening in breathtaking contrast to the darkening sky. She waited patiently and watched the trees and the stray ghost-like cloud pass by overhead, illuminated by the moonlight. It was lonely in the summer when the nighttime arrived and you were alone. They say standing beside the ocean can make you feel small, but staring at the wide-open country sky can do the same thing. Claire was distracting herself with those thoughts when a Mustang sped up in front of her house and screeched to a halt.

The passenger's side window rolled down and Russell was behind the wheel with an arrogant grin. He waved her over and she stood as a foolish adrenaline ran down her legs and arms that pumped from her chest. It was a good rush.

As she climbed in she heard Russell say, "Miss me?" He was three years older and he had a deep, intimidating voice, a thick beard and the build of a burly farmer.

Claire just smiled and buckled her seatbelt.

Russell reached his right hand over and set it on Claire's

thigh. His hand was heavy and made her leg look tiny and she politely brushed it off and smiled and said, "Ah ah ah." He replaced it back on the shifter and they were driving down the road. There was plenty of land around, and they drove for a while and watched the darkness continue to roll in, and when it was nearly black Russell circled the car back to a plot of trees—state land that backed up to Claire's neighborhood. It was a perfect location—it gave the illusion of freedom and independence but with a short drive home, which would be key for Russell after the amount of booze he planned on drinking.

The road ended at a small circular lot of pavement but Russell slowed his car, checked for anyone around, and then turned off the road and onto a path that locals had worn with years of bald tires fueled by raging hormones. It wasn't a particularly smooth path and Claire could hear Russell wince occasionally when they hit a root or a rut in the dirt—a Mustang probably wasn't the best car to bring back there. The path followed a gradual curve through the woods and eventually opened up to a small, sloping clearing. He followed the edge of the trees along the perimeter of the area and when the ground flattened he came to a stop and turned out the headlights. He looked over at Claire.

"How's this?" he asked.

"Looks good to me." There was nervousness in her voice but she played it away with a smile and a wink.

"Good." Russell patted her leg again and then exited the car. He picked through the edge of the woods for sticks and twigs and then tossed them in a pile next to his car, and then he walked over to his trunk and pulled out a few logs he'd split earlier in the day. Claire was now standing against the front of the car and rubbing her arms to keep warm. A late evening cool had settled and the cold metal of the car didn't help. Russell must have seen and reached inside his car to grab a jacket off his backseat, and then he set it over her shoulders.

She smiled politely and thanked him, and then he walked back over to the pile of sticks and continued building his fire. Claire nestled into the jacket and it smelled like campfire and dirt and she was just thankful it wasn't body odor or sweat. For a couple minutes she tilted her head back and stared at the stars. They were beautiful, regardless of how many times she'd seen them. She could watch them glowing, unmoving, for hours and be happy. She always considered them nature's greatest distraction.

When she brought her head back forward she heard Russell mutter a phrase of cheer and a moment later a deep orange flame was burning its way from the kindling and over the thick logs. The fire crackled and the glow lit up Russell's face almost as much as his proud smile. She returned the look.

"There we go!" he said as he walked back toward the car and leaned into the trunk and pulled out two campfire chairs and unfolded them by the fire. Then he went into the backseat and pulled out a backpack and waved Claire over to the fire with him.

"What's that?" she asked.

"Just a little celebratory toast." He had a clear plastic water bottle filled nearly to the top with a brown liquid, along with a liter of Coke. They were sitting now and he unscrewed the caps on each bottle and then took a swig from the liquor and a swig from the Coke. "It's Captain," he said through a strained voice as the residual burn faded down his throat.

He handed Claire the bottles and she thought better for a second but then did the same as Russell. She coughed and spit up a little Coke and gagged but managed to hold most of it down.

He laughed and took the bottles back from her. "Maybe a little more Coke and a little less Captain on the next go." He took a long drink from the water bottle and waited a moment before chasing with just a sip of Coke, which, following her struggle, she took as an arrogant move. She quickly grabbed the bottle of Captain and, ready this time, took a swig and swallowed with confidence and handed it back to Russell.

He laughed and said, "Alright, let's both just calm down here."

She lost her edge then and smiled with him and said, "Thank God because that was the worst thing ever."

"You don't have to drink straight liquor to impress me."

"No?"

"Not at all. You just have to wear dresses like that one."

She could feel herself beginning to blush and then was grateful for the darkness that surrounded them. Regardless, she looked away for a moment to regain her composure.

They sat by the fire for a long while, drinking from the bottle and laughing and telling stories. At one point Russell scooted his chair closer to hers so that the armrests were touching. She let that move go, and then he reached over a few minutes later and touched her arm and she flinched. He removed his hand and took one last long sip and the bottle was nearly empty.

"Can I have the last of it?" Claire asked. But before Russell could answer, they heard the sound of tires coming down the path toward them. It was a gentle sound. The car must have been moving slowly. They both turned and looked but couldn't see any headlights. That worried Claire and she stood up and walked over to the other side of the car.

"What are you doing?" Russell asked in a quiet voice, little more than a whisper.

She didn't respond. Truth be told, she was getting ready to hide, or run, or whatever she needed to do depending on who it was. She was a drunk minor and she wasn't going to let herself get caught.

Just then, a set of blinding headlights flicked on, pointed right at their fire. It was the police. The car stopped and they heard a voice say, "Stay where you are."

Russell listened, but Claire didn't hesitate and ducked into the woods. She didn't think the cops saw her, but she couldn't be sure and so she continued deeper into the forest. She always had a wild side to her, but even she would have been a little uneasy about scooting through these woods at night, were it not for the alcohol and adrenaline pumping through her body keeping her fears of the forest stowed away. It wasn't quite a run, but a brisk pace that she maintained for a solid fifteen minutes until she came to the edge of the woods and realized she wasn't far from her own home. She took a deep breath and the adrenaline let up and the alcohol kicked back in and she heard herself laugh out loud and began a casual stroll toward her house.

2

Her mother was sitting at the kitchen table drinking hot tea when Claire came stumbling through the front door. Claire's inebriation distorted her ability to conceal her slyness and a usual silent slip through the back door and into her bedroom without being discovered was no longer an option for her.

At first Claire didn't see her mother. The lights were off with the exception of a flickering candle in the kitchen. Once inside, Claire tried to quietly close and lock the door behind her and then she giggled to herself again and cupped her hand over her mouth to muffle the noise. When she started forward into the entryway, which led straight a few strides into the kitchen, she raised her eyes and immediately saw her mother sitting patiently staring at her. That was all it took, a simple look, to destroy all of the excitement that she had experienced over the last few hours—and especially over the last twenty minutes.

"Hi," Claire said as a way of starting the conversation. She thought that would be the best course of action—initiating the dialogue. She thought that would put her in control of the situation. But what she couldn't see, and what her mother obviously could, was her slap-happy drunkenness.

"Where have you been?" her mother said plainly. She took another sip of tea.

"Just out, you know." The problem with Claire's proactive plan, other than being too incapacitated to think clearly, was that she didn't actually brainstorm an acceptable alibi.

"Where?"

Claire walked into the kitchen and tried to keep a straight face, but the entire time she wanted to burst out laughing. She flicked on a light and then grabbed a glass from the cupboard and filled it with cold water from the sink. "Just out, with Davey."

"I am asking where you and Davey were."

"We went to the creek. We were fishing." She drank the water and it just kept on going down. She didn't realize how thirsty she was. She finished the glass and then refilled it.

"And how much did you have to drink?"

"What are you talking about?"

"I'm not stupid, Claire," her mother said. The stoic look on her face never fled. She took another sip of her tea and then set it down on the table and stood.

"Okay. Well I'm not drunk."

"How much did you drink?"

"Just a little, okay?" Claire was beginning to cave, but she thought she could still get away with it if she played her cards right.

"Just a little? It doesn't seem like just a little by the way you're rocking against that counter."

"I'm not rocking."

Her mother gave her a skeptical look.

"What do you care anyway? I can do what I want." She was losing her confidence and becoming frustrated. She took another sip and tried to gather her thoughts.

"I'm your mother and I want to know what you were doing. Do you even know what time it is?"

"Who cares?"

"Claire, there's not much good that can happen at this time of night, especially when you've been drinking."

"Please don't lecture me."

"You need to be careful. Take it from me. Don't make the same mistakes that I made."

Claire could feel her face reddening. It felt hot and she felt her heart beating fast. "Oh, what, you mean having me? I was a mistake?"

"That's not what I'm saying, Claire."

"Sounds like it!"

"I love you and I wouldn't change anything in my past. All I'm saying is that things can happen when you're not ready for them to happen."

"I promise I won't fuck Davey, is that what you want to hear?"

"Claire."

"Mom."

"Don't use that language with me."

"I can talk however I want."

Her mother tried to remain calm and keep the conversation focused on Claire's actions and not her swearing. "Listen, a fifteen-year-old girl should not be going out with boys and getting drunk."

"What the hell are you gonna do about it? It's my life!"

"Claire, please calm down."

"No!"

"Do you know how your aunt Chloe died?"

That question took Claire off-guard and she thought for a moment. "Hit and run," she finally said plainly.

"Late at night," her mother added. "And do you know why she was even out walking in the dark at that time?"

"No."

"Because she had a temper, and she got into an argument with our mother and stormed out."

"What's your point? That I'm mad now so I'm going to go running in front of cars?"

"That's not what I'm saying. I'm just saying you need to

keep under control and recognize when you're putting your-self into dangerous situations."

"Yeah, got it. Understood. I'm leaving now." Claire started to walk for the hallway and then her mother spoke again.

"I get it. Drinking is fun." Claire stopped and listened. "Es-pecially when you're a teenager and it feels a little dangerous and cool. I'm not going to punish you for that, okay, I get it. I did the same thing when I was your age. I'm just telling you to be smart about it, okay? Do it safely. I know Davey is a good kid."

"Yes he is," was all Claire said. She felt her heart rate slow-ing and her energy to uphold her anger was dissipating, and she was left with a guilty exhaustion. She gave her mom a sub-tle look of appreciation and then continued down the hallway and into her room. She closed and locked the door behind her and then collapsed face-first onto her bed. The lights were still off and the stars from out the window cast a dim glow in-side. Rolling over onto her back, she stared outside at the trees and the sky and just thought to herself. She knew her mother was trying to do the right thing, the parental thing. She knew it must be difficult to raise a child on your own. Hell, it was hard growing up with just a mother and no father, so she knew that struggle first-hand. It was one that she and her mother both felt. That absence. That loneliness. Like some-thing was missing. She just wished she could do something to fill the void. And so that night for the first time in years—maybe it was the booze, maybe just emotion—she slid off her bed and kneeled on the floor and looked out the window to the stars and prayed.

3

When the sun peeked over the trees the next morning and shone into Claire's room, she was already dressed and slipping into her low-rise Converse All-Stars and heading out the door. She didn't feel great, with the effects of her first hangover surely setting in, but she had a determination that she'd never felt before.

It was a brisk morning and there was a slick layer of dew covering her bike, which had toppled over onto the lawn since the previous evening. She wiped off the handlebars with her shirt, hopped on and began pedaling. The neighbors were slowly making their way outside to their cars to head to work. For the most part, though, the community was quiet and still and she listened to the sounds of the wind whipping past her head as she picked up speed down the sloping concrete. A little further and then she made a turn and kept pedaling faster and she knew she was making good time.

When she saw Davey's house she held her feet still and glided toward his driveway. As the subtle incline of the pavement slowed her pace she swung her right leg over the center bar and in one fluent motion dropped the bike on the lawn and jogged up to the porch. She knocked firmly and a minute later Davey opened it wearing a plain white undershirt and gray athletic shorts. His hair was a mess and he rubbed the sleep from his right eye.

"What are you doing here?" he said groggily.

"What are you doing?" she asked as she pushed past him into the house. "Where's your family?"

"I don't know, at work?" He was still standing by the door with his hand on the knob.

"Seems early to go to work."

"My brother is probably sleeping still or something. Why are you here?"

She stopped and looked him in the eye and with a smile on her face she said, "Are you up for a challenge?"

"What kind of challenge?" he asked with skeptical hesitation.

She stepped over to him and put her hand on his shoulder. "I need your help."

"With?"

"I want to find my dad."

"Your dad. You want to find your dad."

"Yes, I want to find my dad."

"Okay. Where do you want to start looking for your dad?"

"I'm not really sure."

"Okay, good start."

"We'll figure it out."

"How about I go back to bed, and then you wake me back up when you know where you want to start." He turned and started walking up the stairs and Claire followed him all the way into his room, and when Davey collapsed back into his bed Claire sat down at his desk and opened his computer.

"There's gotta be some info somewhere," she said as she opened the web browser.

Davey's face was planted in his pillow but he managed to turn his head just enough to say, "What's the guy's name?"

"I'm not even sure of that."

That answer caused him to sit up on the edge of the bed and say, "How the heck do you plan on finding the guy if you don't even know his name?"

"I don't know. Just help me."

"What do you want me to do?"

"I don't know," she admitted. She was determined, but she was also realizing quickly, as her energy level settled, that this was going to be a difficult if not impossible task.

"Where is this coming from?"

Claire paused for a moment. She was still looking at the

computer, with Davey to her back. "My mom and I got in another fight last night."

"Shit. What happened this time?"

"I don't know. I was drinking with Russell and I came home and she was still awake and knew I was drunk and started questioning me about it. One thing just led to another."

"Well I don't blame her for getting mad about her fifteen-year-old daughter drinking with some eighteen-year-old man," Davey admitted with a hint of jealousy in his voice.

"I didn't tell her that part, duh. I told her I was drinking with you."

He stood up and said, "Why the hell did you do that?"

"It seemed like a better story."

"Why, because I'm safe?"

"Because you're a good guy and she trusts you," Claire said quickly. She turned around and could tell that what she'd said started to calm Davey. He didn't say anything though, and so then she said, "I'm just sick of fighting with her."

"And you think finding your long-lost father will fix the fighting?"

"I just think I deserve both of my parents." She was losing her confidence. Then she added, "If that's even possible."

Davey walked over and lowered himself to one knee beside Claire and placed his hand on her shoulder. "Okay, tell me what you know about the guy."

"You're gonna help me?"

"Claire, of course I'm going to help you."

She smiled.

"I just wish you had decided you wanted to find him closer to lunch time."

This time she laughed and then said, "Well all I know is that my mom didn't know him very well and that after she got pregnant he disappeared."

"That doesn't sound like a great guy."

"Well she said she didn't even get to tell him that she was pregnant, so the news isn't what scared him away."

"Got it. Okay, listen. We don't really have much to work off of here, but I think you deserve to meet this guy or at least find out who he is, so why don't you go home and try to dig up anything you can from your mom and then we can go from there."

Suddenly her enthusiasm and confidence returned and she stood up from the desk. "Deal," she said, and then turned and walked out of his room and down the stairs and out the front door and rode away as quickly as she had arrived.

4

Claire burst through the front door and into her mom's room. She knew her mother would still be in bed, as her hours at work were taking her late into the evenings, meaning a later start time as well.

The room was dark and the blinds allowed nearly no light inside. Claire first called for her mother to wake up and then went to the window and opened the blinds. A rush of light filled the bedroom and her mother rolled over, trying to shield herself.

"Mom," Claire said. "I want to talk to you."

Her mother just made a noise of irritation and remained still.

"Mom."

"What?" she answered groggily. Claire couldn't blame her—she would act the same way were someone forcing her awake. But she was on a mission and couldn't afford the feeling of sympathy.

"I need to talk to you," Claire said.

"About what?" Her head was still buried in the pillow.

"About my dad."

This got her mother's attention, and she rolled over and looked Claire in the eye. "Why do you need to talk about him? And especially why do you need to do it right now?"

"It's time I learn the truth."

Her mother took a deep breath and said, "Go put the coffee on and I'll meet you in the kitchen in a few minutes."

Claire listened and left the room. It was a short walk to the kitchen and she seemed to make it in just a few energetic strides. She'd put the coffee on for her mother many times, so that part was quick and easy. A minute later she hopped up on the counter and folded her hands in her lap and pretended to be waiting patiently, but her heart was racing and her eyes remained locked on the entrance to the kitchen where her mother would surely soon arrive. The sound of the coffee machine gurgling and the smell of the French roast tried to distract her but she nonetheless continued watching the entryway. She felt like a loyal dog, with nothing better to do but wait patiently for its owner to arrive. Now she was swinging her feet and her heels were banging against the drawers below her on the backswing. That's when her mother appeared.

"How old are you? Cut that out," her mother said.

Claire stopped and smiled and waited for her mother, who was just standing in the entryway, to begin talking. She didn't say anything and just looked at Claire for a moment with a blank stare and then walked over to the opposite counter where the coffee was brewing. She stood in front of the machine with her back to Claire and waited for the brewing to conclude. Claire remained patient. When the coffee was done, her mother removed a white mug from the cupboard overhead and poured herself a cup and then motioned for Claire to join her at the kitchen table.

They were sitting across from each other not saying a word. Claire was ready to burst but considered that her mother was gathering her thoughts and wanted to give her more time to think.

"I'm sorry for last night," her mother finally said.

That took Claire back a moment, but she brushed away the apology in hopes to get into the main topic of discussion. "It's okay," was all she said.

Her mother raised her eyebrows, as if waiting for a more thorough response to her comment. She set the mug on the table and ran her hands through her long blond hair, taking the lot of it and draping it in front of her left shoulder. Then she leaned forward on the table and cupped both hands around the warm, steaming mug.

"I'm sorry too," Claire added.

Her mother waited another brief moment, but then must have realized that was the best she was going to get from Claire and moved on. "Where did this need to know about your father come from?"

"Fifteen years of not knowing who he is," Claire said plainly.

"Fair enough."

"So will you tell me?"

Her mother nodded. "I will tell you what I know."

"What you know? Like, you don't know who you had sex with, or something?"

Her mother gave her a look. "That's not what I'm talking about. Claire, you have to cut me some slack here. As tough as it was to grow up without a dad, it was also tough raising a daughter alone."

"Okay."

"Okay, so then where to begin." She looked at the ceiling and thought about the past. "I remember the first time I saw your father. He was very handsome and he had a very modest look about him. He was a quiet guy. Obviously that's not one of the traits you got from him."

Claire could sense her mother wanted the attempt at humor to be appreciated, so she forced a smile. "Good one, mom."

A smile—much more genuine than Claire's—rose on her mother's face. But then it faded and she began speaking again. "The truth is, as you might have guessed, I didn't actually know your father very well."

"I kind of figured. What's the story?"

"Well," her mother started, but then paused and looked away and composed herself. She looked back at Claire and gave her the whole story. "After your aunt was killed, your grandparents and I had a really hard time. We didn't get along, we were always fighting or crying. It was a bad situation. Eventually they thought the best thing would be to move away and try to start new. So that's why we moved up here."

"They moved to Marquette to *avoid* being depressed?"

"Well believe it or not we were all on board for the move. After we got here your grandfather hired a local landscaping company to fix up the yard at the new house." She paused again, as if giving Claire a moment to try to guess what happened next. When she didn't, the story continued. "Your father worked for that landscaping company."

"You got knocked up by a local landscaper?"

"Listen," her mother snapped. "Whatever image of a Marquette landscaper you have in your head, that wasn't your father. He was handsome and sweet and quiet."

"So what happened then?"

"I thought he was cute, and one day when he was done working I asked if he would show me around. That night we did exactly what I told you not to do last night. We drank some liquor and we had sex. I was still an emotional mess and I didn't know what I was getting myself into. He took me home and I didn't think anything of it, other than I wanted to see him again. But when I called him his phone was disconnected. I was mad, but really I was more sad. Anyway, a few weeks later when I learned I was pregnant, I knew it was his—it could only have been his. So I tried calling again, but it was still disconnected. I had to get ahold of him, so I had your grandpa call the landscaping company. They put us in touch with his landlord, but even that old man hadn't seen or heard from him in weeks."

Claire was staring blankly at her mother as she spoke, and her mother must have seen the emotions building inside her daughter and stopped telling the story for a minute. Claire took a deep breath and folded her hands in her lap. Softly, she rocked forward and backward for a moment to try to calm herself, but she could feel herself about to burst into tears at any moment. Instead she tried to speak, hoping the words would force the sadness from the front of her mind. "So he basically slept with you and then left town?"

"Basically," her mother said softly. "And that's exactly why I am so protective over you."

Claire nodded. She understood. "How old were you?"

"Nineteen."

"How old was he?"

"He was twenty-five."

"What's his name?"

Her mother pondered it for a moment, preparing to speak that name she hadn't heard spoken aloud in years. Finally, she said, "Mason. His name was Mason Clark."

"Mason Clark," Claire repeated. "So my name would have been Claire Clark."

"Would have been," her mother said. "But isn't. You're my girl."

"Yes I am," Claire said. She tried to smile but then a tear rolled down her cheek and it just seemed hopeless. "Thanks for telling me all of this, mom."

"Of course. I'm sorry it took this long to tell you the truth. But I want you to know, that as unprepared as I was to become a mother and as unexpected as you were, you are the greatest thing that has ever happened to me."

"Thanks, mom."

"I love you, Claire."

"I love you, mom."

Claire stood up and her mom did the same and they stepped together and embraced. Her mother squeezed her tightly and Claire felt her strength give. For as long as she wanted to know the truth, for as ready as she thought she was, it was painful to hear. When they pulled apart, her mother sat back down at the table and Claire announced that she was going to head to her room. As she turned the corner to walk down the hallway, she looked back to her mom and asked one final question.

"What was the old man's name?"

"I'm sorry?"

"The old man. The landlord. My dad's landlord that you talked to. What was his name?"

"Geez, what was his name?" her mother said to herself as she tried to remember. Then it hit her. "Ah! Last name Jones. Bartholomew Jones, I believe it was. You don't forget a name like that. I remember he hated being called Bartholomew though. Can't really blame the guy."

"I've never met a Bartholomew before," Claire said curiously, and then she turned and headed for her room.

5

She was lying on her bed staring at the ceiling and the thoughts just kept pouring through her mind like a raging river. One thought in particular hit a nerve and she couldn't let it pass.

She was thinking about her father, who he was and where he was and what he was doing. But what haunted her was that he didn't know. He didn't know she existed. He didn't know he had a daughter. Maybe he wouldn't have left. Or maybe he would have come back, had he known the truth. Maybe he still would. No, she told herself then. That's just foolish to think. You have to be smarter than that—or at least tougher. After a little while she rolled over and picked up her phone and called

Davey. Two rings and he answered. He always answered her calls.

"Wassup?" he said.

"I need your help."

"What's going on? Did you find out who your dad is?"

"Sort of. Enough to work from, I think. Can you be here in ten?"

"Ten minutes? No." There was a silence on the line and Claire felt a rush of defeat. "Give me twelve."

She smiled and something told her that he could tell she was smiling. "Deal."

So she waited her twelve minutes. She stood from the bed and walked over to her desk and pulled out a piece of paper. With a black pen from the drawer she wrote "Mason Clark" right in the center of the blank white page. It was flashing in her mind and she needed to see it in front of her—physically see it written out. Somehow, she thought, that would make it more real. Maybe it would make him more real, since all he had been up to this point in her life was a runaway ghost.

She continued to stare at the name, and then she wrote it again. And then again. And then again. And then she set the pen down and looked away and tried to think about something else. That's when Russell came to her mind. She was just realizing that she hadn't spoken to him since the night before when the cops showed up. Grabbing her phone, she sent him a message.

HEY WHAT HAPPENED LAST NIGHT? she typed.

She set her phone down, but seemingly as soon as she did it buzzed. COPS SHOWED UP AND MIPED ME, he sent, referring to the ticket he got for drinking underage.

SERIOUSLY? SORRY. He didn't say anything for a minute. She felt a little guilty that she left him to get in trouble alone, but then she thought that it would have been foolish to have stayed. It's not noble to get a ticket when that ticket could be avoided. Regardless, the guilt remained and so then she sent, WANNA HELP ME DO SOMETHING TODAY?

NOT REALLY.

PLEASE?

NOT REALLY.

YOU CAN HAVE SEX WITH ME.

REALLY?

NO PERVERT.

WHATEVER.

She tossed her phone on her bed, a little disgusted, but then she knew she was asking for that response. It wasn't that she actually wanted Russell to tag along, but she felt bad for abandoning him the previous night. It was probably best that he didn't join, she knew that would bother Davey. She knew Davey liked her, or at least had some kind of protective feeling over her.

Looking back down at the paper, she read the name out loud a few times. Then she wrote the name "Bartholomew Jones" next to it. Then she said that one out loud. It felt strange to her. For a moment she thought maybe she was losing her mind, and then she smiled to herself. And that's when she looked at the doorway to her room and Davey was standing there with his arms crossed and a wide grin.

"So who is this Bartholomew fella?"

"Geez, when did you get here?" Claire asked.

"A minute ago." Davey walked into the room and took a seat on the bed. Claire spun around and faced him. "You gonna tell me?" he continued.

"He's an old man who was also the landlord for my father."

"Is that right?"

"And we're going to find him."

"Is that right?"

"Yes."

"Why don't we just search your dad's name online?"

Claire sat and tried to think of a reason, but couldn't come up with one. She thought she just needed to talk to someone first-hand who knew the man first. "Because that's inefficient. There have got to be too many Mason Clarks out there. Can you just look up the address?"

Davey looked reluctant to retrieve his phone from his pocket, but Claire knew he must have been relishing this moment. "What was his last name, Jones?" His thumbs were moving rapidly on the screen and he was focused, and Claire just sat there and watched, wondering how anyone could type so quickly. "Got it," he said.

"Does he still live around here?"

"According to this, yeah."

"Let's go find him!" Claire jumped from the chair and out into the hallway. Davey stood and followed her out the front door and by the time he could see his truck parked in front of the house, Claire was already sitting shotgun. "Hurry up!" she called.

He couldn't help but smile. She was bouncing in the front seat like a child ready for the amusement park. When he climbed in the car, he said to her, "You need to relax."

"Not at all!"

They started driving down the road. "You gotta think, what if this guy isn't home? Or what if he's dead or something? Or maybe he just doesn't know anything."

"Geez, you're a downer."

"I'm just saying."

"And I'm just saying—let's go!"

Claire rolled down her window and let the air blow her hair around. She tipped her head back and closed her eyes, then she stuck her arm out the window and swam her hand through the air like a dolphin in water. She was wild and beautiful and a little bit crazy, but that's what Davey loved about her.

A little while later Davey slowed on the main road and took a turn onto a narrow pass carved into the trees. Claire suddenly sat up and refocused and Davey looked at her for a moment. "You ready?" he said.

"Is this really the road?"

"I guess."

The truck rattled on the hard dirt surface. He couldn't drive more than fifteen or twenty miles per hour, and he prayed that another car wouldn't be coming in the opposite direction, as the road was only wide enough for one vehicle at a time. The sun was blotted trying to pierce through the thick woods surrounding them, and Davey clicked his headlights on. Neither of them said a word and only listened to the old engine in the truck and the sounds of the forest.

A mile or so in Davey could see there was an upcoming opening and he switched the headlights back off. As they neared it they could tell that it was a significant field. The road took them out of the woods and it cut directly across the middle of the field to the base of a large hill on the opposite end, where two small cabins sat. The grass was shaggy and looked like it hadn't been cut in a few weeks. Davey drove cautiously as they approached the homes. Both windows were down in his truck and the warmth of the sun and absence of any breeze in the secluded valley caused a thick mass of air to roll slowly inside. Finally the truck eased to a complete stop and Davey squinted to read the address.

"Is this it?" Claire asked quietly. There wasn't a sound now and they could hear themselves breathing.

"Yep."

"Then let's do this."

They exited the vehicle and walked over to the larger cabin on the right. The wood looked to be dried and cracking and hadn't been cared for in quite some time. When they reached the stairs, there was an uneasy creaking sound and the wood seemed to absorb their weight to an unnerving degree. They hurried up and each step seemed to echo beneath the hollow porch.

"Knock," Claire said.

"Why me?"

"You're the guy."

"But we're looking for *your* dad."

"Geez, you big baby." She reached her fist out but Davey quickly swatted it away.

"Okay, fine." He knocked three times loudly and then they stepped back and waited. Nothing. So he reached out and knocked again, this time with five strong strikes, and then they waited. They looked at each other and contemplated that he might not be home, or maybe he was just ignoring them, and then the doorknob jiggled and they heard the bolt lock recall and the heavy door seemed to swing open from pure momentum. Once it did, they saw an old man sitting in the entryway in a wheelchair. He had on a denim jacket and his hair was white and messy and the skin on his cheeks was loose.

"Can I help ya," the man said as more of a statement than a question. His voice was gravelly and deep.

"Are you Mr. Jones?" Claire asked.

The man didn't flinch.

"Bartholomew Jones?"

"It's just Jones," the man said. "Can I help ya?"

Claire and Davey shared a quick glance, and then Claire

said, "Jones, I'm looking for someone and I thought you could help me find him."

"Who's that?"

"His name is Mason Clark."

A pale flush came over the old man's face and he looked worried for a moment, and then he put his head down and wheeled forward out the door, splitting his two guests. He rolled to the end of the porch near two chairs with a small table between them. When he stopped, he motioned for them to come join him. They did and each took a seat.

"How do you know Mason Clark?" Jones asked.

"Well," Claire started, unsure how to word what she was to say next. "This may sound strange, or unexpected—it's still weird for me to say—but he's my father."

"Yer father. Is that right." Jones thought for a moment. Then he said, "How old are you?"

"Fifteen."

He thought again. "So yer the little girl. Yer mama came around here lookin fer yer daddy not long after he ran off. That feels like a lifetime ago now."

"Yes, sir."

"What do you want me to do fer ya now?"

"We want you to tell us where Mason Clark is now," Davey interjected, sounding eager to get involved in the conversation. Claire gave him a look, as did Jones.

"I don't know where Mason is now."

"You have to have some idea," Claire pleaded.

"I'd say someplace in Tennessee."

"Why would you say that?"

"Yer a pretty girl. I ought to have known Mason would have a beautiful little girl. That boy was quiet and sure didn't take care of himself, but I always knew he had good genes in there somewhere."

Claire tried to stay on topic. "Sir, please. Why do you think he might be in Tennessee?"

"Well, I got a letter a few years back. Says he was livin in Tennessee someplace. First and only time I heard from him since he ran off—which was outta nowhere, might I add."

"Do you have the address from where he sent the letter?"

"Probably someplace. But it won't do you no good. I wrote him back and got no answer. Doubt he's still livin there."

"But you never know," Davey added.

"Yeah, you never know. True, boy."

"Sir, can you please get me the address?"

The old man looked hesitant now, but he agreed and rolled back inside and was gone for a few minutes. Claire and Davey looked at each other and then looked out at the pasture. Claire looked at the cabin next door, where her father used to live. It was beat up and run down, with leaves and twigs and even a couple larger branches layering the roof. It didn't look like it had been lived in since her father left sixteen years ago.

When Claire's eyes returned to Davey, he had his head down and was typing away on his phone.

"What are you doing?" she asked.

"Searching for anything I can find on a Mason Clark in Tennessee."

"Don't you think you should wait until you have a little more info?"

He looked at her and then clicked his phone off and put it away. "I guess I'm just eager to help," he said.

"I know," she said with a smile and then patted his leg. "Thank you."

Jones came rolling back onto the porch with a letter in his hand. He gave it to Claire and she unfolded it and read it to herself. It was mostly small talk, telling Jones when he got to Tennessee, what he missed about Marquette and the old man's company. But it meant a lot more than just small talk to Claire. She analyzed the handwriting and softly ran her index finger over the ink, hoping that she could touch it, that the letter would somehow offer a physical presence of the man she never knew. It yielded nothing. Her heart felt heavy now and she looked up at Jones and Davey, who were watching her closely.

"Well?" Davey said, raising his eyebrows in anticipation for her response.

She shook her head. "Nothing, really."

"Well here," Davey said, leaning over her shoulder and taking a photo on his phone of the address from where the letter was sent. "Now we at least know one place where your dad was in the last few years."

"It's a start," she said.

"Take the letter with you," Jones said. They looked at him, curious about his request. He must have seen the looks on their faces. "Yes, go on. Take it with you. I hope he's still livin there and you can find him."

Claire was overjoyed and stood and walked over to Jones and leaned in for a quick embrace. When she pulled away, the old man had glossy eyes.

Then Jones said in a broken voice, "If you do find him, tell that son of a bitch he still owes me rent."

6

The left turn signal in Davey's truck was burning out and after he flicked it on to turn back onto Claire's street it clicked rapidly.

"Damn thing," he mumbled under his breath.

"I can't believe it," Claire said, holding the letter in her lap with two hands and staring at it. "I can't believe I just got this."

"It's pretty amazing."

When he pulled the truck to a stop in front of her house, she turned to him and said, "Let's go find him." She had an energetic smile and Davey had a difficult time refusing that look on her face.

"Really?"

"Really."

"When?"

"Tonight."

He laughed that off. "C'mon," he said.

"Seriously!" She pulled the door handle and let herself out of the truck, and then closed it behind her and leaned against the side of the truck and spoke to Davey through the open window.

"You're crazy."

"A little, probably."

"Okay, how about this," he began. "Let me go home and do a little research. If I find anything out about the guy, I'll call you and we'll plan our trip."

She smiled again. "Deal." Then she trotted up the front lawn and into her house. When she reached her front door, she turned around and gave Davey a wave, and he was still sitting idly by the curb watching her. For lack of a better idea, she blew him a kiss and tucked inside. Then she thought, that was probably dumb, but who cares?

Her mother was at work and Claire headed into her room and dropped the letter on her desk next to the formerly blank piece of paper that now had her father's name written all over it. She took a seat and looked at them. Then she unfolded the letter once more and placed it directly beside the other sheet. Her eyes darted from one to the other, comparing the handwriting—hers and his. Maybe there would be a similarity that shouted "I am your daughter!" But there was none. Stark differences in handwriting between male and female, Claire thought. And who wrote in cursive anymore anyway? Her father was undoubtedly from another generation.

Lying back down on her bed, she wondered how long it would take Davey to dig anything up. She pulled out her own phone and held it out in front of her and did a quick search of her own. What came back was limited, with no real juicy information. Nothing to work from, anyway. She clicked her phone back off and closed her eyes. She thought of a world where her dad never disappeared, where she and her mother and father went on family picnics and vacations and watched movies together in the evenings. There was no pain and no confusion or yelling and they all got along just fine. In fact, they smiled. There was always so much happiness and it never went away, even during the bad times, because they always had one another for support. Then she thought, that's just a dream. No family is actually like that. You're just putting these false notions in your head of something that doesn't really exist. And it will never exist, not for you, because once time passes you can never get it back. So your childhood is gone, and he wasn't there for it.

In an attempt to shake the raging thoughts from her head, Claire stood from her bed, undressed, and went into the bathroom to take a shower. The water was hot and steam rose around her and for the first several minutes she didn't even bathe but rather just allowed the water to wash down her body and she breathed in the steam. The entire process calmed her, both physically and emotionally.

After the shower, she dried herself and went back into her room. She decided to put on her Northern Michigan tank top and cutoff jean shorts that she hadn't worn in a while. Her hair was still wet and she pulled it back into a ponytail and then put on a forest green conductor hat and pulled the hair through the back. She looked herself in a full-length mirror on the wall, pivoting from one side to the other to get a full image of her outfit. It would certainly do.

What else was there to do to kill time? She looked back at her desk, at the letter and the paper sitting on it, half-expecting that they would be gone, that the last several hours didn't actually happen and were just in her imagination. She snatched the letter and read it through again. Then she flipped it over and read the return address out loud. Somewhere in Tennessee. Not that she was a bad student, but Tennessee geography wasn't one of her strong suits. So she did another quick search on her phone: WHERE IS MERCY, TENNESSEE?

The map that appeared was far too close and it took her a second to zoom out in order to get a better understanding of where this town was in relation to the rest of the state, or the country, for that matter. The town was on the far eastern side of the state, and then she zoomed back in to see its location in relation to other places she may know. It was southeast of Knoxville and appeared to be a small village tucked in the rolling hills and mountains of Appalachia. It was far from Marquette, but for some reason seemed to make sense that her father would leave Michigan's Upper Peninsula and travel to this place. It looked nearly untouched by man, still a part of God's Country, just like the U.P. She was getting eager to go there.

A couple hours had passed since she parted with Davey and she checked her phone every few minutes to see if he'd tried to contact her, but each time she was disappointed. The day was growing older now, and as evening rolled in Claire finally sent Davey a text.

ANYTHING?

She didn't hear back for a couple minutes and she picked up the letter from her desk and read it again. Then she took her phone and called her mother. She knew her mom was probably going to be working for another couple of hours, but maybe she could catch her on her break. Sure enough, she heard, "Hello?" on the other end.

"Mom?"

"Yes, sweetheart. What's going on?"

"Mom, I found Mr. Jones."

"I'm sorry, who?"

"Bartholomew Jones."

"Oh, honey, you didn't actually go looking for him, did you?"

"Yes, and I found him! He lives in some old shack outside of town in the woods."

"Probably the same place he lived when I talked to him when I was pregnant."

"Probably."

"What did he say?"

"He gave me a letter from my dad."

Claire could hear her mother take a deep breath into the phone. "What did the letter say?"

"Not much, to be honest. But he sent it from some small town in Tennessee."

"Is that right? Is that all the old man knew about where your father might be?"

"That's it."

"I guess we couldn't have expected anything more."

Then Claire announced, "I'm gonna go find him."

"Excuse me?"

"I'm gonna go find him."

"No you're not, Claire."

"Yes I am. I'm going to find my dad."

"Claire, listen to me. You aren't going anywhere."

"He's my dad and if there's any chance he's still in this town in Tennessee then I am going to find him. He's my dad, I deserve to meet him."

"Don't you think I would like to confront the man that got me pregnant? But you can't just go running halfway across the country on a whim because you found a letter that's who-knows-how-old."

"It's from three years ago, and yes I can," Claire said in a calm voice.

Then her mom took another long breath and said, "Listen, we can talk about this when I get home, okay?"

Claire didn't say anything.

"I'll take that as an okay. See you later, sweetie."

Claire didn't hesitate. As soon as the call ended she quickly called Davey. He picked up on the second ring.

"Hey, sorry I didn't respond to your—"

"Don't care," Claire said firmly, cutting him off. "I'm taking off for Tennessee and I need you to come with me."

"What? Claire, don't you think that's a little premature of you? We don't even know—"

"Not at all. Are you coming?"

"I think you should think this over a little longer."

"Meet me at the Speedway by my house in thirty."

"Claire."

"Be there."

She hung up the phone and then sat down on her bed. She let out a couple deep breaths and tried to slow her heart rate. She needed to calm herself and refocus. Once she felt composed, she grabbed a duffle bag from her closet and started packing. Only the essentials, she thought. Pants, shirts, toiletries, some cash, a bottle of vodka from the cabinet and a book she found on her mother's bookshelf called *A Land More Kind Than Home*. She wasn't exactly sure what it was about, but she knew it took place in the Appalachian Mountains and the title seemed appropriate for her situation. Then she slid back into her All-Stars and out the door. She made sure to leave in plenty of time. She didn't want to leave her bike at the gas station, so she would have to walk. The street was dark and there was a soft glow from the bright moon overhead that reached the pavement to light her path. The gas station was about a ten-minute walk, and she took her time. When she stepped under the Speedway lights she looked around but didn't see Davey's truck. She continued over to the convenience shop near the pumps and was just about to walk inside for some road snacks when she saw Russell through the window. He was walking toward the checkout counter so she stayed where she was outside the door. Unsure of his feelings toward her, she decided it was better to wait and have him run into her, instead of vice versa.

A minute later, the little bell on the door rang and Russell stepped outside. He looked right at Claire, who was standing on the small curb waiting for Davey to arrive. Russell smiled and she knew immediately that he was drunk.

"Well hey," he said. He walked over to her and gave her a hug.

She would have been happy to see him if he were sober. "Hi," she said. Then, plainly, she said, "Drunk again?"

He must not have picked up on her voice inflection, because he said, "Me too!"

"I know. Didn't you just get an MIP?"

"Yeah, so?"

"And you're drunk again anyway?"

"I was sad that I got in trouble, so I decided to get drunk."

There was nothing brighter than that logic.

"You look cute," he added. He still had the sloppy smile on his face.

"Thanks."

"So, what are you doing here?"

"Waiting for a ride."

"Where you going?"

"Tennessee."

"Tennessee? Why are you going there?" Now he was over-enunciating everything he said in an effort to sound less drunk-off-his-ass.

"To find my dad."

"Your dad is in Tennessee?"

"Hopefully."

"May I join you on your quest to find your dad in Tennessee?"

"Sorry, Davey is taking me." She could see the disappointment on his face. So she added, "If he ever shows up."

"Please, let me join you."

She thought for a minute and then said, "I tell you what. If Davey doesn't show, then you can. Once you're sober, that is."

"That sounds swell!" He leaned against the side of the building, which he probably thought looked casual, but in reality just made him look even more drunk.

The two stood there, not saying much, and waited for

Davey to show up. After a good half hour and no Davey, Russell finally said, "Can I join you on your quest now?"

"Not yet."

He huffed and then went back inside to use the restroom. When he came back out, Claire was still standing in the same spot on the curb with her duffle bag slung over her shoulder.

"He's not coming," Russell said.

Just then, Davey's truck came speeding up and screeched to a halt in front of Claire. He rolled down his window and apologized. Then he said, "And I still think this should be thought through a little better, but I'm in."

"Too late, man," Russell called. "She's going on her journey with me!"

Davey gave Claire a look that said, "He can't be serious."

Claire admittedly would have preferred to go on the trip with just Davey, but the teenager inside of her that was still upset he took so long to show up wanted to teach him a lesson.

"You're both coming," Claire said, and walked around to the other side of the truck and climbed inside.

"No way," Davey said, but Russell was already hopping in the backseat of the crew cab.

"Let's do this!" he called.

"Shit," Davey mumbled

Claire smiled with amusement at Davey's displeasure, and it wasn't until after they were already about an hour on their way that she realized inviting Russell was a bad idea.

7

It was dark for many hours as they drove through Wisconsin, Illinois and Indiana, but Claire didn't mind as she never thought there was much to look at in those states. They were pretty flat and the bright lights and tall buildings of Milwaukee and Chicago never impressed her. She didn't want to sleep either, though, because she was guilty about Davey having to drive his truck. But deep down she knew he wouldn't mind.

They had stopped once for gas already just before crossing into Illinois, and Claire ran inside the station and paid for the fuel. She was a little upset that Davey didn't thank her for doing that, but then she figured he had a right to reserve his gratitude for a later time when he wasn't being used.

Russell was passed out in the back seat about an hour into the trip and he didn't wake up until they were already in Indiana, except for some stirring and repositioning. By the time they were nearing Indianapolis the sun was back over the horizon and it shone with a blinding glare into the driver's side of the car. Davey squinted and put on sunglasses and tried to block it with the built-in visor over his head but it all just added to the distraction that the sun brought.

Claire was finally nodding off as the sun warmed her skin through the window, and that's when they felt a jolting thump from under the car. Davey gripped the wheel fiercely and Claire reached out for anything she could hold onto. The car slowed immediately, as if on its own, and Davey eased it to the shoulder.

"Was that a tire?" Claire asked.

Davey was visibly upset. "I don't know. I think so."

"What's going on, guys?" Russell said leaning into the front seat. He rubbed the sleep from his eyes, which only half-opened.

"We think we just got a flat tire," Claire told him.

"Shit." Russell looked around and then offered a wide yawn and finally said, "Alright, well let's take a look."

He hopped out of the car and Claire and Davey watched him slowly circle the vehicle, his head down examining the tires the entire time. He brought his fist to his chin and pondered the damage for a moment, in very serious thought. Then he approached Claire's window and tapped tightly with the back of his index finger. She rolled it down.

"What do you think?"

"I think the front right tire is blown," he said with a smirk. "You got a spare for this thing?"

"Under the bed," Davey said.

"Alright."

Davey and Claire shared a look again, this time more a shocked expression that Russell was actually being useful. They watched as Russell retrieved the spare tire and carried it around to the busted one. He knelt and got to work, taking off the current tire and replacing it with the spare. At one point Claire looked over at Davey and whispered, "Do you know how to change one of these?" to which Davey shook his head sheepishly. For the most part they remained silent. It took about five minutes in all—obviously he had done this before. Russell tossed the blown tire in the back seat and then rubbed his blackening hands together.

"I think I have a rag back there," Davey said.

"Thanks."

Russell snatched the rag and did his best to wipe his hands clean. He spit into them and rubbed them again and watched the blackness turn to a slimy liquid, but not really get any cleaner. When he climbed back into the car, he suggested that they pull off at the nearest exit and find a place that can throw a new tire on.

"I really appreciate the help with that," Davey said.

"Yeah, Russell, we wouldn't have been able to change that

if you didn't come along with us."

"It's no problem," he said. He gave Claire a wink and then she turned back around.

Davey was careful with his driving once they were back on the highway. Even with his emergency flashers on, he drove slowly in the right lane and they watched cars come up fast behind them and then swerve over and fly by. Claire didn't say much. She felt her phone vibrate in her pocket and it was her mom, again, for the seventh or eighth time, warning her that she better come home soon or she'd call the authorities. Claire ignored the threat and set her phone to silent. She was distracted by the flat tire for a while, but then her thoughts returned to her father. She imagined what it would be like to meet him. What would he look like? How would he take the news? Would it be a happy moment or a sad one? She tried to imagine the best possible scenario. They pull up to his house and knock on the front door and he answers. Their eyes lock for the first time and no one needs to say a word because they just know. And they embrace and she feels for the first time what it is like to have a father. It's the greatest moment of her life.

But then her mind reverts to pessimism. She imagines finding the house and knocking on the door and the owners answering and telling her that they've never heard of Mason Clark and that they've lived there for twenty years. She realizes that her father used a random and false address to send the first letter. He doesn't want to be found and he's doing a pretty damn good job of making sure it stays that way.

She felt a rush of adrenaline quicken her heart rate and warm her face. A minute later they were off the highway and pulling into a tire shop. Davey left the truck running and went inside for a minute, and then he came back out with an attendant following. The man inspected the other three tires and then told Davey that they had the same model on-hand. Davey asked how much it would cost and winced at the price, but reluctantly agreed. The three of them went inside the shop and waited in uncomfortable chairs beside a coffee table covered in magazines for about fifteen minutes. The entire time Davey looked sick to his stomach. Russell was smiling to himself and reading Sports Illustrated and Claire reached over to Davey and patted him on the shoulder.

"I'm sorry about this," she said softly, with as much sincerity as she could offer.

"It's not your fault, shit happens," Davey said.

When the mechanic was finished replacing the tire, Davey paid the man and they were back off for Tennessee. Claire offered to drive and before they entered the highway she put another tank of gas in the truck. Davey was reluctant, Claire only being fifteen and without a license, but he was tired and trusted her to handle the drive. He rested his head against the window and less than a half hour later Claire could hear him snoring. A few hours later, they were driving through Tennessee and Claire stopped to put more gas in the truck.

"Should have rented a frickin Prius," she said to herself.

"I promise you I would not have joined if you were riding in one of those things," Russell said out the window as Claire pumped the fuel.

"Oh well," she said with thick sarcasm.

"You would have been shit outta luck when your little Prius tire blew," he added.

She didn't respond and then climbed back in the driver's seat and continued on the trip. Davey wasn't quite out, but his eyes were still closed and his head was tilted back. The landscape gradually changed as they headed eastward and Claire wanted to nudge Davey and have him look at the view with her, but she refrained and decided it was better to let him socialize on his own terms.

It was early afternoon and the green hills were growing with each mile. They drove between two mountains with rocky sides, and the road had evidently been built with the help of several dynamite blasts. The truck in front of her had a Confederate flag decal covering the entire back window and Claire knew they were in a land much different than the Upper Peninsula. When she passed the truck, the man was wearing a camouflage hat and his lower lip protruded with tobacco, and he nodded a kind gesture as they locked eyes. She continued down the road and it sloped downward and then climbed again and Claire marveled at the mountains all around her. They passed through Knoxville and once they were heading south the mountains before them were majestic and green and daunting yet calming to a girl from the rural

Midwest.

"Says the next exit is it," Davey said.

"About time," Russell added from the backseat.

Claire continued to listen to Davey's directions. They veered off the highway and then continued straight onto a county road. There were only two lanes and very little room for a shoulder before a thick forest approached. The road bent and wound through the trees, and it dropped down the side of a mountain and then back up to a ridge where they looked out over a rolling field filled with grazing cattle.

"Right up here," Davey said.

Claire made the turn and the road seemed to drop steadily downward until it plateaued at the bottom and followed a calmly puttering creek. There were a few houses, every few hundred feet or so, usually tucked back off the road up steep gravel driveways. The homes were built into the side of the mountain and the three of them all rolled down their windows to stick their heads out and look up at the houses. They were quaint and old and unique and full of character. Claire pictured her father living in one of them. In a quick flash her mind went back to the house that her father lived in when he was in Marquette, and she thought about how, despite the sizes of the surrounding mountains in Tennessee, the areas and homes were quite similar to one another.

The car was crawling down the road, which was barely wide enough for one car to pass. If another came in the opposite direction, they would have to pull onto the small line of grass that ran along the road until the oncoming vehicle passed. The road snaked a little farther and then crossed a small wooden bridge to the other side of the creek, and then it bent left and the forest opened up and there was a dark brown log cabin sitting on a small mound a ways ahead. The land around them was green and glided gently toward the trees that surrounded the field. Claire stared at the home before her as they approached. There wasn't any doubt in her mind. This was the place.

8

Claire took a minute, after the car eased to a stop in front of the house, to compose herself and gather her thoughts. She'd come all this way, and she hadn't even rehearsed what she would say to the man who was, hopefully, standing behind that door. Davey and Russell didn't say a word. They watched Claire stare at the house, and then they looked around the area and up at the house as well.

The home was small and looked like it couldn't hold more than a couple rooms. The shingles on the roof were worn and tattered and a single metal chimney spout rose from the back corner. There was a small porch built onto the front that looked like the newest addition, the wood a brighter and healthier color than the rest of the home. Claire wondered if her father had built that himself.

Finally, after several minutes, Davey broke the silence. "Gotta do it at some point."

"I know. I just need a sec."

"Take all the time you need," he said, patting her on the shoulder.

She gave the home one final, powerful stare and then took a deep breath. "Okay," she said. "Let's do this."

"You want me to come with you?" Davey asked.

"Why not?"

"I don't know, I just figured if it's really gonna be the first time you meet your dad and all..."

"And all what?"

"I don't know. I just thought you'd want to do it alone."

"So you're not coming?"

"I'll come," Russell said from the back seat.

Davey shot him a glance. "No, I'll come with you," he said.

"Can I still come?" Russell asked, half-heartedly.

"No," Claire said, and then she and Davey exited the truck and made their way up the gradually sloping path that led to the front porch. With her first step onto the wooden surface the board creaked and she hesitated for a moment, but then continued onward. There was a thick smell of pine that hung in the air. When they were standing beside each other in front of the door, they shared a glance. Davey must have seen the terror in Claire's face, because he lightly rubbed her back between her shoulder blades. It was a comforting gesture and she breathed deeply one more time.

Then she knocked. The solid wooden door gave an eerily loud sound that they could tell resonated throughout the inside of the house. They took a step back and waited a moment. Claire's heart was racing and she felt sweat building at her hair line and on the end of her nose. She tried to calm her nerves with mental strength but the effort wasn't making much of an impact. After about a minute of silence, she knocked again. They waited some more, and as the time passed her heart rate began to slow.

Finally Davey said, "Try again, but I don't think anyone's home."

She knocked again, this time even more loudly than before.

"If someone's home, they would be hearing this."

Claire didn't want to admit it, but Davey was right. "One more time," she said after another minute, and then she pounded with the butt of her closed first. Her anxiety was turning into frustration and without saying anything to Davey she turned around quickly and walked with angry steps back to the truck. She climbed into the passenger's seat and crossed her arms. Davey followed casually and got in the driver's seat.

"So no one home?" Russell asked.

Claire didn't acknowledge his comment.

"Wanna wait it out a little?" Davey asked.

"Sure."

The time passed and they sat in a deadly quiet truck. The radio was left off and with the windows rolled down the sound of the light breeze passing through the leaves of the forest was the only sound. The afternoon was crawling by and after about an hour of sitting Russell couldn't take it anymore.

"What are we doing? The guy's obviously not home."

Davey looked at Claire. When she looked over at him he was giving her a look that agreed with Russell's comment.

"You wanna give up too?" Claire said to him.

"Nobody's giving up, Claire," Davey started. "It's just been a long trip and I think we should go find some food and a place to stay and regroup. Maybe we can figure out where he is if we rest a little."

She reluctantly agreed and Davey turned the truck around in the grass and started back up the hill and through the woods and back out onto the main road. He made a right and followed the road for several miles until they found themselves eating at a McDonald's, and then a half hour later they were standing in the lobby of The Mercy Motel. It was a dated one-story motel with about forty rooms that each opened to a long outdoor walkway.

"One room or two?" Davey asked as they pulled into the lot.

"I'd love to say two, but can we afford that?" Claire asked.

"Well, I can afford my own room and you guys can figure

out the rest."

"That works for me," Russell interjected.

"No," Claire said. "Let's all just share one. Just for a night or whatever."

"Okay, so how is this gonna work. I mean, the sleeping situation?" Davey asked.

"I get a bed," she started, and then she couldn't help but smile, "and you two can share the other."

"Fuck that," Russell said.

"Then get a cot, I don't care."

"Whatever," Davey said. "We'll figure it out. Let's just get a room."

There were a good number of cars in the parking lot so they had the initial thought that the motel might be low on rooms—which surprised them, given its isolated location in the mountains. The little lobby at the end of the motel had a few sitting chairs, a wooden fixture that held pamphlets for local tourist activities, and a single desk with an outdated desktop computer. They stepped inside and were looking around when a woman stepped out from a room in the back to greet them.

"Evenin, y'all," she said. She had thick glasses and a nearly floor-length dress on. Her hair was short and curled and she looked like she could have been sixty, but Claire guessed she was more like fifty.

"Hello," Davey said. "We'd like a room, please."

"No problem. Just one fer the three of y'all?"

"How much are they?" Claire asked.

"I can git y'all two rooms fer fifty."

"Damn, okay. We'll take two, then," Claire said.

Davey turned away from the woman and looked at Claire. "Two rooms? So how is this gonna work?"

"I don't know, but it's cheap enough. Better than someone on a cot."

He nodded, though his question was still unanswered. Claire had an accurate feeling that both of her male companions had their eyes on her room. She imagined Russell stepping forward and honorably sacrificing himself to share a room with Claire, selflessly offering Davey his own room. And to that gesture Davey would politely decline and tell Russell that he was more than welcome to take the solo room to himself and he would reluctantly share with Claire.

Davey was talking to the woman again, paying her, and getting their room keys. "And I expect full reimbursement for this, guys," he added.

They left the office and went back to the truck. Claire grabbed her bag, as did Davey, and then the three of them walked across the gravel parking lot toward the two rooms, which were down near the end of the building. There was a dusty substance that sat on top of the gravel and as they walked it chalked the sides of their shoes and puffed into the air. Russell was empty handed, having spontaneously, and drunkenly, joined their excursion.

"Think we could find a Walmart or something around

here?" he asked.

"Why? Because you decided on a whim to drive two thousand miles?" Davey said.

That comment unnerved Russell a little. "Something like that," he said as calmly as he could.

When they got to the rooms, as if right on cue, Russell said, "Listen, Davey, thanks for shelling out for the rooms. It's only fair you get your own for doing that."

To which Davey responded, "It was no problem. You can take the single room."

Claire offered to bite the bullet that seemed to be burdening her friends. "Guys, I'll take the single room. It's no problem, I'm happy to do it." She said it with a straight face, though she was smiling wide inside. She wanted to watch their faces, see how they reacted, but instead snatched a key from Davey's hand and unlocked her room and closed the door behind her. Pressing her ear back against the closed door, she listened to the conversation that ensued.

"Way to go," she heard Russell say to Davey.

"Fuck off."

"Whatever, I'm gonna go find some booze."

Claire peeked out of the front window, through the white curtain, and watched Russell walking away, across the parking lot, toward the gas station next door.

It only took Claire a minute to completely collapse. She hadn't noticed until this moment, but she was exhausted. The drive, the anticipation, the letdown—it had all built into an overwhelming fatigue and she found herself sprawled on her back, lying on the bed, staring at the ceiling and thinking about her life. Maybe it was a mistake, driving all that way to end up in an outdated, dirty motel in the Smoky Mountains. Her mind trailed back to that home, to sitting in the truck and watching it just sit there, in front of her, a taunting arrogance that she was alone and that her most anxious question will never be answered. Then she was standing on the porch again. She closed her eyes. She pounded on the door and her fist went through it and then she looked inside and saw her mother's house, the house where she was raised. And everything her mind told her led to some kind of familiarity, that this place was somehow connected with her, that the trip was not all for naught.

Suddenly Claire's eyes sprung open and she was still lying on the bed. She thought for a minute that she had fallen asleep, but then she thought that she hadn't. One of those inconclusive moments in life. Unknowing and uncaring, she rolled off the bed and went into the bathroom to shower. She turned on the faucet and then watched the water pour from the spout with a decent pressure. She undressed and kicked her clothes toward the door and then felt the water temperature before stepping in. She adjusted the knob a touch toward the warmer side and then she was in the shower. The water ran over her body and to complement her exhaustion, she realized how badly she needed this shower. Her hands ran over her hair and nearly came out slimy from the grease. But to her surprise, she didn't really care. She stood for a moment and let the water run down her body before cleaning herself, and then she exited the shower and dried herself off and casually got dressed in cotton shorts and an old t-shirt that she'd packed. Standing in front of the over-sized bathroom mirror, she looked at herself. Her hair was still damp and black and hung in front of her shoulders and down her chest. She teased it a moment and then decided that she had indeed fallen asleep on the bed before, and that nap and the shower were enough to give her a second burst of energy, so she grabbed the bottle of vodka that she'd stolen from her mother and slipped on her sandals and left the room. She walked down the walkway outside to the office, where the ice machine was, but the door was locked. She tried to see inside the dark room but no one was present. Reluctantly, she headed back and stopped outside Davey's room.

Claire only had to wait a short moment before Davey answered her knock. He looked frustrated. Claire raised the bottle of vodka and smiled and it seemed as though Davey was trying to force a stoic look, but then cracked and smiled and invited her in. "Russell still out?" she asked, and Davey just nodded. She grabbed the two plastic cups, individually wrapped in baggies, that were sitting beside the bathroom sink and poured a little vodka into each. She smelled the liquid and it stung all the way up her nostrils and into her eyes. Her eyes felt watery and she tried to blink the feeling away. Then she stuck the cups under the sink and filled them the rest of the way with water.

"Cheers," she said to Davey after she walked back over to the bed and handed him the drink. They bumped the cheap plastic cups together and then took a sip. Claire winced. Even with the water, it was still far too strong. Davey didn't react, but then set the drink down on the side table and said, "God, that's awful." But he smiled after he said it and that made Claire feel better.

"Definitely," she said and returned the smile.

They sat and drank slowly while they talked, and then Claire refilled their cups and they continued for a little while longer. It was a pleasant night and out the front window they could see the darkness in the sky and the one bright street light that hung over the parking lot. Davey was sitting on the edge of the bed and Claire crawled to the top and rested against the headboard. She felt so comfortable around Davey. He was a sweet kid who always meant well, and who treated her like an angel. She took another sip and pictured them back at the creek fishing, turning her head and catching Davey staring at her. Why did she treat him the way she did? Taking advantage of him? Asking outrageous favors because she knew he couldn't say no? It was unfair of her, but she liked the way he needed her. And she thought, just maybe, that a part of her needed that too.

"I'm sorry for making you come all the way down here," she finally said in a quieter tone when she was almost done with her second drink. Her head was a little woozy now but she was feeling extreme relaxation, despite the hard, springy mattress.

"Don't apologize, Claire. I'm glad I came down here."

"Really?"

"Of course. You know, other than the flat tire, all the gas, the time away from work and the motel rooms, it's been great." He smiled to let her know he was just kidding, and she returned the look but knew that what he'd said was true. She'd put him through an awful lot already, and nothing had been accomplished.

"I'm really glad you came with me." There was a sincerity in both her voice and the way she was looking at him. All he could do was smile and take the final sip of his drink.

"Another?" he asked.

Claire nodded, but before she could roll off the bed for the refills, they heard a rustling outside and then suddenly Russell came bursting through the door. Both Claire and Davey froze and stared at him. He just stood in the doorway for a moment, and it only took that long for them to note how intoxicated he was.

"Are you two drinking?" Russell asked.

"Looks like you've been drinking," Davey noted.

"Yes, I have been drinking. What's it to you?"

"I was just saying—"

"What were you just saying?"

Realizing that Russell had a much shorter fuse with the booze in his system, Claire jumped in and said, "Alright, guys, relax."

"You guys are drinking in here without me?"

Instead of answering, Davey simply asked, "Where have you been drinking?"

"With some guys I met."

"Some guys you met?"

"Did I stu-stu-stutter?" Russell said with slurred speech.

"At the gas station?" Claire asked.

"Yep!" He smiled and looked so proud of himself. Then he added, "Let's take some shots!"

"I don't think so," Davey said.

Russell walked over to the vodka bottle and when he tried to grab it off the table, Davey snatched it away.

"Give me that shit," Russell said.

"No."

"Give it to me." He leaned over and grabbed the bottle, and they played a short game of tug-of-war before the much bigger Russell eventually won and seized the bottle. Davey didn't look defeated so much as angry. "Now let's take shots!"

"No," Davey said sternly.

"Piss of, little boy." Russell took the empty cup on the table that had previously been Davey's and poured a little of the vodka into it. "Anyone?" he asked open-endedly.

They didn't take him up on his offer and he downed the first gulp, then poured another. Claire looked at Davey, whose face was reddening. He got up and walked into the bathroom, for just a moment, and then returned slightly calmer as Russell took down another shot.

"I'm going to bed," Davey announced.

"But we're drinking," Russell said.

"No, *you're* drinking," Davey said pointing at Russell. Then he made a motion with his hand between himself and Claire. "*We're* not drinking anymore."

"C'mon."

"Sorry."

Claire was a little surprised by Davey's announcement, but then it made sense. She figured it was her fault. She allowed Russell to join them on their trip, even knowing how Davey felt about him. Her heart was beating quickly. Davey sat down on the edge of the bed.

"Fine," Russell said, and then grabbed the bottle and walked out of the room.

Claire gave Davey's shoulder a soft rub and said that she'd had a really good time talking with him. She offered a genuine smile, just a soft one to let Davey know she meant it, but he was still angry and didn't seem to acknowledge her.

When she exited the room, Russell was waiting on the walkway. "Wanna drink a little more?

"Not really."

"C'mon, don't tell me you're tired and going to bed too."

The truth was she wasn't tired and certainly didn't want to go to bed. Between the adrenaline pumping from the previous confrontation, to the alcohol, to the thoughts still running through her mind about her father, she was wide awake. She didn't want to tell that to Russell, of course. But she gave in, slightly, and said that she'd sit outside with him for a little while. They walked over to Davey's truck and unlatched the tailgate and sat down. Russell's feet could touch the ground but Claire's just dangled in the air. She felt like a child sitting next to a grown man when she was around him sometimes.

"More booze?" he asked and put the bottle in front of her. She politely declined and felt it was better not to tell him that it was her bottle and that she didn't want him to drink it anymore. She said nothing and he took another drink.

She was surprised at how calm he was being. Maybe the short conflict with Davey used all of his energy. Or maybe the excess amount of alcohol that he'd consumed was playing a role. Regardless, she was okay with it. They talked casually for a little while. It was dark out and the one light in the parking lot barely reached the truck. When they looked out at the road and the forest beyond it, all they saw was darkness. Claire yawned and thought about turning in for the night, and that's when Russell made his move.

"I'm tired," she said, and in one motion he set the bottle down and leaned over her and kissed her. It happened so fast and his momentum dropped her back flat on the pickup bed. She felt her tooth go into his lip but he didn't seem to notice. She pushed him away but it took him a second to restrain himself. When he lifted off, he was hanging above her and staring into her eyes.

"What the hell!" she said, shocked and angry.

"What?" he said, surprised by her disapproval of his action. "I thought you liked me?"

"I don't want to get into this right now," she said, trying to push past him and sit up. The look on his face washed from confused to nearly furious in an instant. He put his large hand on the center of her chest and pushed her back down to the metal surface. Suddenly a wave of fear and anxiety rushed through her. "Don't do this," she heard herself saying to him, as controlled as she could, while he breathed heavily over her. She thought he'd start foaming at the mouth. "Please," she added, and felt a tear coming to her eye.

For a few more moments neither changed positions, but gradually Russell's breathing slowed, and as it did so did hers. Finally he removed his hand and sat upright and reached for the bottle. Without looking back at Claire, who was still lying on the truck bed, he said, "I'm sorry." He took another swig and then Claire sat up.

Her fear mutated into her own form of rage. "Give me your room key," she said flatly.

He pulled it out and handed it over to her, still not looking her in the eye. She took it and hopped off the tailgate, and then left her room key where she'd been sitting. "Sleep it off," she said, and this made him look over at her, perhaps surprised that she was acting so cordial toward him. But when their eyes finally locked, she narrowed her gaze and said, "Don't ever fucking touch me again." And then she left.

9

Davey was fast asleep when Claire entered the room. He didn't even flinch as she kicked off her shoes and flicked on the light in the bathroom. When the light went off she walked slowly, feeling for the bed with her outstretched arms in the dark. There were two beds in the room, but she found the one where Davey was already sleeping and lifted the covers, still fully clothed, and crawled in. She scooted herself across until her body pressed against his back. He flinched and was suddenly awake, but she wrapped her arms around him and clenched as tightly as she could, and when he realized it was her he relaxed and held her arms. She brought her face to his ear and opened her mouth to whisper her gratitude toward him, but nothing came out. Davey must have felt the warm breath on his neck and rolled over to face her. He put his hand to her cheek and felt a cool wetness. He reached over and flicked on the lamp beside the bed. That's when he saw the tears in her eyes. He asked what happened, but she just buried her face in his chest. That's how they slept for the next six hours.

— — —

The sunlight lit the white curtains in the morning and they seemed to glow. Claire groggily opened her eyes and Davey was already awake staring at her. She was instantly wide awake, yet both her mind and body were completely drained. He looked like he was waiting for an explanation, but she offered none.

Rolling over, she climbed out of bed and headed into the bathroom. Splashing cool water on her face, she stared at herself in the mirror. Her eyes were still red and bloodshot and she had a drowsy sag beneath them. She rubbed them for a moment but that only made it all worse, so she splashed some more water on her face, dried off and then went back out into the room.

Davey was sitting up in the bed in just an old white undershirt and athletic shorts. "Good morning," he greeted her.

"Morning."

He raised his eyebrows and kept looking at her. She knew

he was waiting for an explanation, but she really did not want to give one. She would force him to actually ask before she offered anything.

He said, "So what happened last night?" He looked like he wanted to smile, but refrained from doing so, most likely knowing that it wasn't anything positive that made her come to him last night.

"Russell kept drinking and just turned into an asshole."

"I could have told you that was going to happen. Where is he now?"

"My room. I traded him keys. I had to get away from him."

"Why didn't you just go back to your room?"

It was a straightforward and fair question. Claire couldn't think of a good reason. She was drunk the night before also. She wanted to get away from Russell, sure, but did part of her want Davey to comfort her? It was true he had always been there for her. Why else would she climb into bed with him? She needed his support, because Russell wasn't just being an asshole, he crossed a line. But she couldn't tell Davey that, he'd flip his shit. Finally, Claire said, "I don't know, to tell the truth."

Davey couldn't hold his joy in any longer and a smirk appeared on his face. "Well you certainly surprised me."

She looked at the carpet and was a little embarrassed.

"In a good way," he added. He walked over to Claire and lifted her chin with two fingers and looked her in the eye. "I mean it. It was a good thing."

She smiled for him, but she wanted to cry. There was a tightness in her chest when she thought about Russell the night before, lying powerless beneath him. The alcoholic breath in her face. That look in his eye. She was helpless and knew it could have been much worse. Now she thought she might actually drop a tear so she looked over at the wall, away from Davey. Then she reached for her phone on the bedside table and saw several messages and missed calls from her mother. Her troubles were piling up and she laid her body down on the bed and stared at the ceiling. Her arguments with her mother. Her failing search for the man she'd never known and who she was now beginning to believe she would never know. And then Russell. There was a burning feeling behind her eyes and she thought that maybe it was the tears building up, and that when she sat back upright they would all come spilling out.

Davey was in the bathroom brushing his teeth. The door was open and Claire could see inside. When he was done, he spit and rinsed and wiped his mouth with a hand towel, which he then slung over his shoulder as he walked back out into the room. "You know," he started, "I really don't think Russell should have come with us."

It was an obvious statement. "Maybe you're right," she said, but she knew he was definitely right.

"Nothing we can do about it now, though."

"You're right again."

Claire was still wearing the same shirt and cotton shorts

from the night before. Her bag with a change of clothes was in the room next door, with Russell, and she decided she would rather continue wearing a dirty outfit than knock on his door.

She rinsed out one of the cups from the previous night and then filled it with water, but when she took a drink she could still smell the vodka and almost puked. Instead, she just cupped water from under the bathroom faucet and drank it that way. Davey was squatting in front of the TV stand, where, on a lower shelf, there was a small coffee maker. The machine was gurgling and Davey waited patiently for the cup to finish brewing and then took it. He added a couple packets next to the machine and stirred them in, and then he blew on the surface and took the first sip. He winced, seemingly from both the temperature of the coffee and the taste. Claire knew he wasn't much of a coffee drinker, though she would admit she didn't know many sixteen-year-old boys who were.

Now she was standing next to Davey, and when he looked at her she said, "Are you ready?"

"For?"

"To go find my dad again?"

"Oh. Yeah, let's do it." They headed for the door and once outside Davey stopped and gestured toward the other room. "You gonna wake him?" he asked.

"Nah." She shook her head. "Judging by last night, he'll need to sleep it off."

They crossed the parking lot toward Davey's truck. The tailgate was still down and he threw it back up and then they both climbed inside. Claire apologized for leaving it down and then explained how she and Russell had been sitting on the tailgate talking and when she left to go inside he must have forgotten to put it back up. Davey nodded in acknowledgement of her explanation but didn't seem to care too much for it, and then they started driving. Claire was happy they were leaving Russell behind, and she knew Davey must have been thrilled. At one point on the drive, Davey even said with a smile on his face, "Maybe we can just leave Russell down here when we go home," to which Claire smiled and nodded in agreement.

There was still a morning fog that had settled over the road and Davey had a difficult time seeing ahead. He drove slowly and Claire stared into the fog and tried to picture where the road was going to turn next, but it was like staring into an endless glow. The windows were rolled down and the moisture seeped inside the truck. Claire ran her hands over her hair and then put it up on a ponytail. Above them they could see the sun trying to shine through the thickness of the clouds and fog. The road bent to the left and then curved back upward to the right. At the top of the hill they looked out over a green valley that was choppy and wavy, and as the fog settled on top of it like a whipped cream topping and they both realized quickly why these were called the Smoky Mountains.

There weren't many other cars, which was good considering the low visibility level, and they continued to wind through the hills and mountains, Davey and Claire straining to remember the right path, until eventually a little while later they found themselves descending back into the same holler as the previous day. They crawled along the narrow road until they arrived at that same house. It looked just as quiet and peaceful as the day before. Davey brought the car to a stop and they sat in silence for a moment and looked at it, then around the property. It was beautiful, they could offer that much.

After a minute Claire said, "Wait here," and then walked up to the porch and knocked a few times. She tried to peek through the front windows but no one was answering. Then she climbed off the porch and walked around to the back of the house. A minute later she returned to the truck and told Davey that she was positive no one was home. "And I'm not sure anyone even lives there, judging by what it looks like inside," she added.

But they had driven a long way and decided to wait a little longer, just to see if anyone showed up. After a couple hours, they left and drove back toward the motel until they found that same fast food strip, ordered some greasy chicken and fries, and then returned to the house in the early afternoon. This time, as they pulled up they noticed another truck was pulled up and parked right next to the porch at the end of the driveway. They froze and Davey stopped his truck when they saw it. They looked at each other. Claire's heart was pumping and she didn't wait for Davey to pull any closer, she just opened her door and headed in a purposeful pace toward the porch. Davey quickly killed the engine and followed her, barely closing his car door behind him.

Claire was on the porch now and she was pounding with decent force on the front door. Davey hopped up next to her, and just as she did the door opened. They both stared nervously. A middle-aged woman answered. She was wearing a nice blouse and khaki pants and flats. Her hair was long and straight and she wore thick-framed glasses.

"Can I help you?" the woman asked.

Claire was shocked to see a woman, and tried to look past her into the home to see if anyone was with her. Davey recognized the awkwardness of Claire not responding and stepped closer to her and said to the woman, "Hi, we're looking for a man named Mason Clark. We were told he lived here."

"Ah, yes," the woman said. She adjusted her glasses on her face. "Mr. Clark was the previous resident. How do you know him?"

"He's my uncle," Claire lied. "It's been a while, though. He usually comes up to Michigan to see us, but we wanted to come down and surprise him."

"Well that's nice of y'all."

"Would you be able to tell us where we could find him?"

"Can't you call him?"

"We could, but like I said we're trying to surprise him. I guess we're gonna have to call him if you can't tell us, though."

The woman thought for a moment, and then retreated into the home. They could see her leaning over a table about twenty feet inside, facing away from them. Without looking up, she called, "What were your names?"

"Mallory and Jones," Claire called inside. She glanced at Davey, who was looking at her like she was crazy. She gave him a look that said she knew what she was doing.

The woman returned with a small piece of paper, and proceeded to hand it to Claire. She looked down and there was an address written in fine black ink. "That's his new address, not too far from here. Just up the road a piece in another holler."

"Thank you so much, ma'am," Claire said sprightly.

Davey offered an excited smile as well and then they both turned and headed off the porch. Claire stole a quick peek at the woman's truck and noticed a "Bergman Realty" sign painted on the driver's side. They had missed her father, but not by much, and now they knew where to find him. A conclusive address. In her hand.

— — —

That moment she had been waiting for was finally about to arrive. Claire's stomach tossed and turned with the truck as they winded around the mountainous terrain. The reality of the situation was finally hitting her. Part of her never thought it was a realistic possibility to find her dad, that she was just using this trip as an excuse to detach from her life for a little while. She didn't think it would actually happen. But now there she was, sitting in the passenger's seat in a truck headed directly for the man who she could call father.

"How you doing?" Davey asked without taking his eyes off the road. He must have known, without a word being said, that she was nervous as hell with a blood pressure through the roof.

"Just trying to keep myself together."

In an effort to distract herself, she took out her phone. It was about to die. She once again had several notifications from her mother, which she continued to ignore. Then she typed out a quick text to Russell. GOT MY DAD'S REAL ADDRESS AND GOING TO FIND HIM. BE BACK LATER. Then she put her phone in the center console and her thoughts returned to her father. What would he look like? What would she say to him? "Hi, I'm your daughter who you didn't know existed." No, that probably wouldn't work. But how to lead into something like that? There can't possibly be an easy way. She could beat around the bush, but then why? She'd come thousands of miles to find the man she had been dreaming of meeting her entire life. Why couldn't she just come right out with it?

But her thoughts were interrupted by an approaching home. Davey was driving slowly now. They were deep in another valley, the road narrow, similarly to where they were before, with tall trees overhanging the path through the forest, and Claire couldn't stop staring at the house. It was sitting alone. Her heart rate began to steadily increase. Davey glanced at her. She looked scared to death. And that's exactly how she felt.

The home was set at the front end of a piece of property, near the road. Davey pulled his truck in front of it, mostly off the road onto the grass. The engine rumbled as it idled. That was the only sound. The sun was hidden behind the hills in the valley and it was much darker than it was before the road descended. A sharp light lined the tops of the trees and then fell into a soft glow to offer just enough dawn before additional lighting would be needed. Claire took a deep breath.

"You ready?" Davey asked.

"I'm not—" Claire began to say, but at the exact same time they saw an old Buick come around the side of the house and out onto the road. It was heading back the way they came. Davey looked at Claire with a shocked look on his face, but Claire was already pointing back down the road. "Go! Follow that car!"

Luckily the truck was still on and Davey whipped it around in the quickest three-point turn he'd ever made, and he was heading back up the road. It seemed to narrow with every mile-per-hour that Davey increased. He was clenching the wheel with both hands and he began noticing how dark the sky was becoming.

Claire was leaning forward with her hands on the dashboard. "Come on!" she yelled. Davey understood the urgency, but he didn't say anything, just continued driving as fast as he could. The hill sloped upward at a steep angle and once they were to the top and had pulled out onto a slightly wider road, Davey saw the Buick. He sped up behind and began following it. He realized quickly that he was a poor driver for a situation like this. There was probably a stealthier way of going about it, but he thought it was too late. He slowed down slightly but Claire just yelled, "Faster!" and he pulled back up close behind the Buick. Davey's chest felt like it was going to explode and he just prayed the cops didn't come across him tailing this car. He also prayed the person driving the car didn't have a temper or a firearm.

A few miles down the road, the Buick's taillights lit up a blinding red and it came to a halting stop on the side of the road. Instinctively, Davey did the same and pulled up behind it. He didn't know what else to do. He wished he would have had more time to think over his decision, but it happened so fast. And the quick thinking didn't stop there. Once completely idle on the side of the road, the driver of the Buick stepped out of the car and began toward Davey's truck. The man was tall and burly with wide shoulders. His hair was shaggy and fell out beneath the raggedy baseball cap he was wearing, and a relatively thick beard covered his face and down his neck.

Claire stared at the man but she couldn't get a good look at his facial features. Her heart was racing, and so was Davey's. They both just sat still and watched the man approaching, and then Davey flicked the locks for additional security. The man stepped up to Davey's window but didn't knock. He just stared from under the low brim of the cap, until finally Davey made eye contact with him and made a face that questioned the man's motives.

"You following me?" the man said sternly.

"What? No," Davey said, cracking the window.

Claire remained silent. She was looking at the man's eyes. They looked fierce. There didn't seem to be any joy in him. She tried to tell herself that this might be her father. She and this man might share DNA, but then she told herself no, that wasn't possible. From one look, and one question that he uttered, she knew they couldn't be blood. At least she prayed to God that was the case.

"Sure as shit seems like you're following me," the man continued. "You were in front of my house and now you're parked behind me on this road."

Davey knew pulling over was a bad call, but he panicked. He tried to save his ass with a convincing excuse. "Just thought you might be pulling over because of car trouble or something, is all."

"Is that right?" the man said skeptically. "The car's running fine."

"Are you Mason Clark?" Claire found herself shouting across the car at the man as abruptly as the thought crossed her mind.

The man took a step back with a concerned look. Then he said, "See, I knew you were following me."

"So you are Mason Clark?"

"What's it to you?"

"We're from Michigan," Claire started, and the man's look

lost its hard edge and found a terrified expression. "And my mom is Mallory Simon."

The man looked alarmed for a moment and took another step back. He turned around and brought his hand to his mouth, and then he crouched to the ground and dipped his face downward. Claire felt like her chest was about to explode. She unbuckled her seatbelt and looked at Davey, whose eyes had just left the man and came back to Claire. They shared an anxious look. This is it. This is the moment.

The man stood and looked at them again. He pivoted his body and lifted the back of his shirt. There was a shiny black pistol tucked into his waistband. The fierceness was back in his eyes and he looked past Davey and said directly to Claire, slowly and clearly, "If you try to follow me again, I will not hesitate to pull the trigger." Then he turned and walked back to his Buick, climbed inside and sped off down the road. Davey didn't move, and neither did Claire, and with the petrified silence that fell over them she could almost hear the splash of the tear as it dripped from her cheek and landed on her arm.

10

For a while, she cried.

She and Davey didn't speak for the entire drive back to the motel. There was the silence and the rumbling of the old truck on the rough rural roads, and there were her thoughts. She saw that man. She kept seeing him, again and again. That look he gave her when she uttered those words. What he heard struck a chord. It was something familiar to him, but from a distant past that he probably never expected he'd encounter again. The past he was running from. But he was just a man, a stranger. That couldn't be her dad. At least that's what she continued to tell herself as Davey pulled the truck into the motel parking lot.

Russell was sitting on the pavement against the wall outside her room. When he saw the truck, he stood to greet them. When Davey and Claire approached, he said his apologies, which almost seemed sincere. Davey didn't want to include Russell back into their evening, but Claire reluctantly forgave him and the three of them went out and got some dinner. Russell talked about what he had done during the day while they were gone—a lot of walking, thinking, watching TV—and then did his best attempt to pry out of them what they did. Davey told the story about going to the house, waiting for a while, and then meeting the realtor and realizing that the house they'd been staking out was not in fact Claire's father's. Then he told the story about going to the new address, but no one was home.

"Geez, I'm sorry to hear that," Russell offered, and Claire gave Davey a look of gratitude for not telling him the whole truth.

When they returned to the motel, it was dark and they filed one by one into Davey's motel room. Claire had remained mostly quiet, still thinking about that man, but her thoughts had shifted from sadness to anger. She could feel adrenaline pumping through her chest, a tightening in her stomach. She knew Davey must have noticed her behavior, but he was kind enough to not say anything. The entire experience earlier in the day had been traumatizing for him as well, so he had stayed fairly quiet as well. Claire was sure the lack of energy and emotion from Davey and her was probably messing with Russell's head, making him believe that they were being reserved because of his previous actions. He was overly thoughtful to the point where it was actually beginning to irritate Claire. So at some point early in their visiting, she stood from the bed and asked Russell for her room key back.

"You want to sleep back over there?" he asked.

"Yep. I'm just tired so I'm gonna go to sleep early."

"Okay," he said and slipped her the key. She forced a smile and said her goodnights and then left. She stopped outside of her door for a moment and took a deep breath of the cool night air of the mountains. It seemed to cleanse her lungs and she did it a second time before heading back inside.

In truth, she was exhausted. She had not lied about that. However, she had no plans on going to sleep just yet. Her right hand was tucked in her pocket and when she stepped up beside the bedside table, she removed it to reveal a set of car keys that she had swiftly snatched a little while before. Then she headed into the bathroom and turned on the shower faucet and let it warm and then stepped inside. For the second time, she could feel the oily sweat running down her body. All of that stress and emotion ran down the drain with it. After the shower, she picked out a fresh shirt and shorts and then laced up her Converse. Glancing once in the mirror, just a quick check that she was presentable, she gave herself an OK and then snatched the keys and as covertly as possible headed back outside into the darkness. She walked the perimeter of the parking lot, staying out of the one overhead light, to remain in the dark until she reached Davey's truck. And then she fired it up and was gone.

On the drive, there was already a thin layer of fog settling into the valleys between the mountains and Claire thought for a short while that it might rain. But she was an outsider and she didn't really know what the weather might do next. She tried to clear her mind, or at least focus it, as she drove. She thought about what she might say to that man. She would tell him the truth, again, and this time force him to face it. Then she could learn her own truth. She would get the answers she had waited fifteen years to hear and had driven thousands of miles to find.

Eventually she pulled up in front of the small cabin in the holler and she stopped Davey's truck exactly where he had stopped it the last time they had been there. Killing the lights, an eerie darkness and silence fell around her and her chest caught with a hint of fear as she breathed. Then she mustered the courage to leave the truck and walked by moonlight up across the front lawn, which was mostly dirt grown over with patches of untamed grass, and then up the front steps to the door. She took a deep breath and knocked three times firmly. She waited. She could hear the knocks echo inside the cabin. It made her feel very alone and she was beginning to think that coming here alone at night was a bad idea, that she'd let her emotions get the better of her and she should turn and run. But her legs didn't move and she waited and then knocked again. Again, no one was there. He was sleeping, she told herself, and walked around the side of the house to try to see inside the windows. This is idiotic, she told herself, but continued anyway.

The build-up and letdown of arriving at the house came and went and she headed back to the truck and sat silently in the driver's seat with the window down. A cool night breeze seeped inside and she closed her eyes and let it wash across her face. It was calming as she listened to the silence. Out of her window she could look upward and see the stars. Millions shone brightly with the absence of city lights drowning nature away, and for a moment she felt as if she were parked on a back road in the U.P. and when she was ready to go home all she would have to do is head a few miles down the road.

An instant later that feeling passed, because a distant sound stole her attention. A bright light flashed in her rearview mirror and she saw the car coming toward her from behind, and when it was near enough it angled around her and pulled to the rear of the cabin. Claire's breathing quickened and she hopped back out of her truck and toward the front porch once again.

She waited. A moment later that same man appeared. From what Claire could see in the moonlight he was drunk. He was wearing the same clothes as earlier, but his posture slumped and he no longer looked angry, just tired. Claire tried to speak, but in the moment she couldn't find any words. The man saw her, acknowledged her presence with a slight hesitation in his walk, and then continued right past her. Claire could smell the alcohol.

"What are you doing here?" he asked with a gravelly voice without turning to face her.

Once again, Claire tried to speak but couldn't make her mind up with what to say. She drove all the way over here with a plan—she was going to be forceful and upfront—but it was failing miserably.

"You alone this time, or is that kid in the truck?"

"It's just me," Claire said in a soft voice.

The man stopped at the door and looked back at Claire. He rolled his eyes and let out an exhausted breath. "You have some questions for me?"

She nodded.

"Come on, then." He walked inside and left the door open behind him. She thought about turning and running, but seemingly without control of her own body she walked forward into the house and closed the door behind her.

The cabin was dark and Claire stood in the entryway trying to adjust her eyes, but she couldn't see anything until the man flicked on a light across the room. It appeared the place was one big room, the kitchen and living room all in one, with two doors in the back wall that she presumed were the bedroom and bathroom. There was little furniture with only a couch and a small kitchen table. The man opened the fridge and grabbed a beer and then asked if Claire wanted one. She politely declined and he twisted the lid off of his and took a swig.

He said, "Sit down," and held out his hand to offer her the couch. Claire sat at the far end and found herself using exceptional posture, which she chalked up to the nerves. The man grabbed one of the wooden chairs at the kitchen table and pulled it up near the couch and sat down. The light was shining from the kitchen behind him and it left a shadow covering most of his face. It was unnerving to Claire and she tried not to look at him. After another sip and a moment of silence, the man said, "So, what are you here to ask me?"

Claire gathered her thoughts and her nerves. Then she said, "Why did you do that earlier, when I told you who my mom was and where I was from?"

"I think we both know why."

Her eyes fell to the floor.

"I suspect there's only one way you could have found me," he started. "That bastard Jones is still alive, isn't he?"

She nodded.

"And he showed you the letter?"

She nodded again.

"Damn that old man. I never should have sent that letter," he said out loud, though he didn't seem to be speaking to Claire.

"You're my father." She said it plainly, looking directly at the man. He didn't flinch. She let the statement hang in the air for a moment. Then she continued. "My mom told me the whole story. The local landscaper. That night. Then never being able to contact you again." She said it all as if they were facts, but there was still some uncertainty in her voice. She needed his confirmation.

"I had to leave."

When he said that, it was like taking her first deep breath. Some sort of burden had been lifted. It was the truth she'd desperately sought for so long. She just wished the feeling that overcame her would have been different. This was her father, sitting directly in front of her. Mere feet away. She'd imagined this moment since she was a little girl. She would smile and run at him and jump into his arms, and he would embrace her with a fatherly grip that said he never wanted to let her go again. But that wasn't how it happened, and Claire didn't even feel the need to stand. She guessed that was real life. It wasn't the fairytale in your head. She felt a tear pushing at the back of her eye and tried to hold it in. "Why?" she asked.

He ignored her question. "God, I can't believe I have a daughter. I can't believe you're sitting right here." But he didn't stand either. There was no conviction in his voice. They continued sitting and looking at each other, and then around the room. He took another drink from his beer.

"Can you tell me why you had to leave?" Claire asked again.

"No, I can't. And you should probably leave."

She was caught a little off guard by his request. "What?"

"Listen, I want to feel grateful that I have a daughter, but the truth is, this news is tearing me apart."

The tear dropped down Claire's cheek and she tried to wipe it away quickly and stay strong. "What are you talking about?"

He finished his beer and stood and retrieved another from the fridge. He opened it and took a long drink. Then he stepped back to the chair he'd been sitting in but stood behind it, resting his offhand on the backrest. "You said your mother told you the whole story."

She nodded. She wanted to say something but then remained quiet and waited for him to continue talking.

"Did she tell you how our only date ended?"

"She said you slept together and then you dropped her off and she was never able to get in touch with you again after that."

"Right, but did she tell you anything about how the actual date ended? Or why it ended, I guess."

She shook her head. "I guess not. Why? She said something that forced you to run away?"

There was an uneasiness about him. He nodded but took a moment to think about what he was going to say. "Your mother told me about her sister."

"Chloe? The one who was killed?"

He nodded and then his face lost all color and his eyes looked dead. "Yes," he said. "The one I killed."

11

She didn't hesitate. It was all one motion—she stood from the couch and was out the door, in the truck, and speeding around the foggy curves of the mountain roads. Her mind was going a million miles a minute. She felt like she was living a nightmare. It was hazy. It couldn't be real. She would wake up in her bed in Michigan and this whole trip would be made up, a figment of her imagination. She didn't have a father. He didn't exist. She lives with her mother, her only parent.

When she got back to the motel she sped into the parking lot and slammed on the breaks outside Davey and Russell's room, spitting gravel into the side of the building. She thought she switched off the ignition but she was moving

quickly and couldn't be sure, nor did she care. She was pounding on their door and sobbing and a couple seconds later a
scared Davey opened the door and she threw herself into his
arms. He cradled her head and she was gripping him as tightly
as she could. Walking backward, Davey eased them over to his
bed and they sat down on the edge, but Claire still didn't raise
her head. He tried to caress her in a comforting motion.

"What's going on?" he asked calmly. "It's okay. It's okay.
I'm here."

She cried for another minute and then she raised her eyes
to meet Davey's. They were bloodshot and puffy. "I went back
there," she said, sniffling. "I went back to that man's house."

"Your father's?"

"Don't call him that!" she cried.

Just then, Russell came bursting through the door, stumbling against the TV stand. "What the hell's going on here?"
he said, visibly destroyed again by booze. Davey shook his
head at Russell's inebriation and returned to comforting
Claire. Russell regained his balance and then said, "Don't
shake your fucking head at me!"

"Will you relax," Davey said. "She's obviously upset."

"Don't tell me to relax either!"

Russell stepped toward Davey. Davey's reaction startled
Claire. Without hesitation, Russell grabbed Davey's shirt and
yanked him upward, and then tossed him across the room.
Clearly outsized in the fight, Davey couldn't even catch his
balance and fell hard against the floor. Claire froze. She didn't

know how to react. Tears were still falling down her cheeks.

"Get up!" Russell shouted.

"Don't!" Claire yelled, but it was as if Russell didn't hear her. He walked over to Davey, who looked injured, and picked him back up by his shirt and dropped him on the bed. Then he stood over him and gave a strong right hook to his jaw. Claire could hear the crack when the fist made contact and she let out a scream. "Stop it!" she cried again. But Russell cocked his hand back and caught the defenseless Davey on the cheekbone. A stream of blood was pouring from his mouth and he howled and grabbed his face as he rolled over onto his side. Claire finally stood and ran over and laid her shoulder into Russell. She knew it wasn't her strength but his drunkenness that knocked him over, and he tumbled to the floor. Then she saw the look in his eye and she turned and ran.

She was out the door and running across the parking lot. She just kept running. She wasn't sure where she was running, but that wasn't even a concern. She could hear Russell's footsteps in the gravel lot chasing her and her breathing intensified and she found herself coming to the road and she ran along it for a moment and then peeled off into a dark field beside the motel. The footsteps chasing her were getting closer and closer and her tear-filled eyes were bouncing in fear and she couldn't see straight as she ran.

Then she thought she heard Russell's voice, but before she could even try to decipher what he said she was lying on the ground and he was on top of her. It took her a moment to come to her senses. She could feel his hands groping her and she tried to bat them away, but then he struck her with the back of his right hand and she clutched her face and continued balling. Russell grabbed her shirt and effortlessly tore it straight down the front.

"Please, stop," she was saying through choking tears.

"You little bitch," he said again. There was an evil in his voice and he slapped her again. She let out a scream that carried across the empty mountains. Then he reached for her shorts. He didn't even search for the button. He was pulling and yanking them with everything he had. The strained fabric cut into her skin and she screamed again. "I said shut the fuck up!" And he raised his hand to strike her a third time, and that's when she heard the voice across the field.

Her face was against the dirt. She tried to adjust her vision and she thought she saw a figure coming from around the side of the motel. It was dark and she squinted but that only made her sight worse with all of the tears. But Russell had stopped his assault. He was in motion to stand when the figure was close enough to throw a punch and send Russell tumbling into the dirt beside her. She scrambled to crawl away and when she felt she was a safe distance she looked back. There was a man on top of Russell wailing on him. Right hook, left hook, the beating was steadfast and angry. It went on like that for another minute as Claire tried to regain her composure.

Suddenly she heard the sound of sirens and she waited another moment and she could see the flashing lights on the road. Looking back at the beating, expecting it to come to a halt, she was surprised to see it still occurring. The man was tireless and fierce. Russell lay beneath him, no longer fighting the attack. A squad car appeared then and pulled off the road toward them and quickly came to a stop. A floodlight lit up the field and Claire covered her eyes. The man beating Russell had his back to the cop, and then the officer stepped out of his car and drew his firearm and yelled, "Police! Show me your hands!" A second officer exited the other side of the car and followed the first's lead.

But the man continued his beating.

"Police! Show me your hands! Get off of that person!"

But the man continued his beating.

"We'll shoot!" the lead officer yelled. "Get off!"

But the man continued his beating.

The two cops gave a couple more warnings but the man's assault never even slowed. They finally opened fire and put several rounds into the man's back, and his fists didn't stop swinging until the final one. He toppled over onto Russell. Claire stared in disbelief. The tears stopped pouring and she could no longer feel her body. The cops, guns still drawn, walked cautiously toward the man they shot and examined him. Then they pulled the man off of Russell. And in the powerful shine of the police cruiser's high beams she got a clear look at his face.

It was him.

12

For Claire, the majority of the night was spent at the police station. It was a small building in the heart of nearby Mercy, which consisted mostly of a small diner, a gas station and a rustic furniture store.

Around six in the morning, Davey walked through the doors and joined her in the uncomfortable chairs in the waiting room. He was hunched over, his lower lip bulging and his right eye nearly swollen shut. Claire's concerned look alerted Davey to let her know he was okay, smiling through the wounds.

"I'm okay," he said. "Seriously."

Claire tried to smile in return but nothing came. She knew

he wasn't okay, but it was kind of him to act that way. He'd just spent several hours in the nearest hospital making sure his face wasn't caved in. "Good," she said.

Davey sat down next to her and put his arm around her. A firm embrace pulled her closer to let her know he was there for her. She breathed deeply and then held in the air for a moment, pretending for an instant that the world stopped moving with her lungs. But then she deflated once more and the weight of the situation returned.

"You okay?" he asked.

"I don't know," she said honestly.

"What the hell happened?"

It was a rhetorical question, she knew, but for reasons unknown uttered, "God knows."

"Oh," he said, digging his other hand into his jeans pocket. "I brought your phone."

He handed it over and she took it in her lap but didn't look at it. "Thanks." A little time passed and they sat like that, listening to the sounds of the small police department in the early morning. Finally Claire said, plainly, "I don't think Russell's gonna make it."

"Shit, are you serious?"

She nodded. She was surprised at her lack of compassion. Even for a scumbag. When a life left the world, especially one who she knew, she thought she'd feel more emotion. But the truth was she didn't feel any.

"Claire, I'm so sorry for everything that happened."

"It's not your fault."

"I should have fought harder against him coming down here with us."

She turned her head to face him. "It's not your fault. Honestly. It's mine. I never should have come down here at all."

"But to find your father," Davey said, and she couldn't tell if it was meant to be a statement or question.

"I already told you, don't call him that."

The phone was still in her lap face down and she picked it up. The screen was black and she didn't know if it was dead or just off. She tried the button and it lit back to life. Once it was fully booted up, a cluster of notifications jumped onto the screen—every one of them from her mother. For a moment she contemplated calling her back. At this point, why not? She never thought she'd miss her mother so badly.

Just then, the decision was made for her. The phone lit up with her mother's face and Claire answered the call after a couple rings and breaths.

"Mom," she said.

"Claire? Sweetie, where are you? Are you okay? I've been calling you and texting you like crazy and you're—"

"Mom," Claire said softly. She could tell her mother was alarmed by her tone.

"Yes? What's wrong, honey? Are you okay?"

But Claire couldn't find any words to say. Suddenly tears started pooling in her eyes and sliding down her cheeks. The phone still to her ear, she tried to turn her face away and wipe the tears with her shirt. She was embarrassed, and for some reason she cared. "Mom, where are you?"

"I'm in the car driving. I got a call from the police late last night. They told me the story. Claire, I'm so sorry. But I'll be there today, okay?"

"Hurry."

"As fast as I can, okay? Just be strong."

"I love you."

"I love you, too. Stay strong, sweetie."

Claire hung up the phone, wiped a few more tears, and then collapsed again onto an unsuspecting Davey who was slouched in the chair next to her with his head tilted back toward the ceiling.

"All good with your mom?"

"She's coming down here." Her voice was muffled in his shirt. Davey didn't respond and then closed his eyes. Claire thought about her father. Sitting in his living room. Watching the words come out of his mouth, as if they were tangible, escaping by the syllable in slow motion, and each one punching her in the gut. She wanted to vomit. The memories of Russell groping her. That rush of nausea returned and she winced. She could feel Davey glance down at her but he didn't say anything. Those bullets, their echoes ringing in her ears. They were so close. Piercing into her father's back—anyone's back. The pain she felt, like they were hitting her. Then numbness.

A stray tear fell onto her bare leg and she quickly wiped it away. She wanted to tell Davey the whole story, about what her father did, about why he ran. She wanted to spill every detail because she wanted someone else to understand. But each time she went to open her mouth, something stopped her, a gagging feeling at the back of her throat as if someone was tugging on her uvula.

Footsteps approached and when she looked back up, there was an officer standing before them. He was holding a case folder and he had a stern yet sympathetic look in his eye. She recognized him. He was one of the officers who pulled the trigger on her father.

"Miss, I'm sorry for what you had to go through last night."

"What happened to that man?" she found herself asking.

"Well, miss, the victim—"

"I'm not talking about him. He was no victim. What about the man you shot? What happened to him?"

"Well, that man, as you are aware, resisted our commands to cease his assault on the—" The officer paused, conscious of how he would reference Russell. "On the eighteen-year-old man, at which point we were forced to use our firearms."

"And he's dead?" Claire asked as a rush of guilt found her gut, a consequence of the hopeful feeling that accompanied her question.

"And that man has since deceased from those gunshot wounds," the officer finished. Then, as if anticipating a downhearted response from Claire, he added, "But let me tell you something about that fella, off the record. He was trash, a wanderer. He didn't have any friends in this town and he sure wasn't goin out of his way to make any."

"But he saved me." She wasn't sure why she said that.

"Well, call it the only good he had left in his heart. Probably been savin that up for a while now."

Claire nodded, and then the officer excused himself back down the hallway. She watched him as he walked away, replaying his words in her head and thinking it was altogether possible that everything happened for a reason.

The End.

Made in the USA
San Bernardino, CA
14 March 2017